The Cat Lady Special

BY D. C. GOMEZ

D. C. GOMEZ

Other Books by D. C. Gomez

DEATH'S INTERN-
BOOK 1 IN THE INTERN DIARIES SERIES

PLAGUE UNLEASHED-
BOOK 2 IN THE INTERN DIARIES SERIES

FORBIDDEN WAR-
BOOK 3 IN THE INTERN DIARIES SERIES

THE ORIGINS OF CONSTANTINE-
AN INTERN DIARY NOVELLA

And a Children's Series - Charlie's Fable

Charlie, what's your talent? - Book 1

Charlie, dare to dream! - Book 2

Table of Contents

Dedication

This book is for four amazing friends who have changed

my world and I deeply respect and love:

Drake, Dana, Maria, and Cassandra.

Thank you for everything.

Chapter One

The forty-five or the pills? Why was it taking me such a long time to pick one? It wasn't like I had that many choices left. I decided this morning I was going to end it today, so why was I dragging my feet? I was broke, about to lose my childhood home, had no food but plenty of bills—enough to wallpaper my whole house. To make matters worse, I was alone, depressed, and the laughing stock of my town. Granted it wasn't like Sunshine, Texas was a huge metropolis. But all one-hundred and fifty-three residents knew all about how my husband left.

To add insult to injury, he quickly moved on with his life. I was replaced, or the popular term lately—upgraded—by a twenty-four-year-old blonde who recently graduated from art school with a pair of double Ds. There was no way I could compete with that, even if I wanted to. I was forty-five, had no formal education, no career, and no potential prospect for marriage. All I had left was my reputation of being a good southern lady. Last time I checked, one's reputation didn't pay for milk, or electricity for that matter.

Okay Angela, make a decision.

I had been telling myself that for the last two hours. Even killing myself was driving me insane. I just didn't want to be a hindrance anymore or a disappointment to Mother. I needed to make a decision. According to the Internet, poisoning was the way most women did it. Did I honestly want to die slowly? To be sitting on my couch wearing this old nightgown counting the minutes until death took me? Negative. That took pills out of the equation.

Then, it hit me. The decision was made. My trusty Smith & Wesson M&P45 would do the job. I loved this gun, so it was only fitting that I use it. It would be a fast death, and a clean one. I just couldn't be shaking when I did it. It had to be one shot, straight through the mouth.

"Meow," Clyde complained from across the table. Clyde was

one of my rescued American Short Hair cats. Clyde and his sister Bonnie were my only companions.

"Maybe I should give you guys the pills first. That way you don't end up in the pound," I told Clyde and Bonnie.

Clyde and Bonnie sprinted away towards my bedroom on the left side of the house. Whoever said cats didn't understand humans had never met mine.

"Fine, after I'm gone, just pray Mother finds you first and not the cops," I yelled at the cats from the living room. They were not moved by my threat. "Just don't eat my face if you get hungry. You have plenty of food in your feeder."

"Meow," one of them replied. I had a feeling it was Bonnie. Clyde would eat my eyeballs if he ever got too hungry.

Did I change my life insurance?

Why did our minds bombard us with questions when we faced death? I was pretty sure I had everything changed. The last thing I needed was to leave those two villains anything after my passing. Oh wait, there was nothing left. The bank was getting ready to take the house if I didn't start paying on the loan I took out. I had been stalling for a while now. My life wasn't getting any better, and it wasn't going to.

I took a deep breath and grabbed the Smith & Wesson.

"I love you daddy. I will see you soon," I said my last words to my dad and put the gun in my mouth.

Ring. I froze. Was that my door bell?

On a Monday morning in early October, it couldn't be anyone important. I took the gun out of my mouth and waited for the pesky intruder to leave. The last thing I needed was some stranger calling the police when they heard gun shots inside my house.

Ring, ring.

They were not leaving.

"Aghhh," I whisper-yelled to myself. I didn't have a choice. I had to go open the door, otherwise the person on the other side would just keep ringing the bell all morning.

I dragged myself off the couch, my gun hanging from one hand. My bare feet slapped the floor as I stepped towards the door. I finger combed through my hair. It had been one of those mornings I hadn't even brushed my hair. Surely, I looked even worse than I imagined. A southern lady would never open her door looking like that, but I didn't care. I'd be dead soon enough, so what difference did one more insult added to my already long list of failures make?

Even though the front door was less than twenty feet from the couch, I moved slower than molasses dripping from a countertop. By the time I reached the door, the bell had gone off three more times.

Planting a frown on my face, I opened the door. "Yes?"

"Hi Ms. Angela," said Julio from the threshold. He stood next to his brother Hector, who waved at me in greeting.

The boys were fraternal twins. Technically, they weren't really boys. If I remembered correctly, they were seventeen, but to me, that was still a boy. Julio was the sweet, well-mannered one who always had neatly-combed, short brown hair. Hector was the little rebel. His hair ran longer at the ends, and he spiked it up in a sort of Mohawk. However, both were about five feet five with the biggest brown eyes I'd ever seen. It was nice being able to look them in the eyes without getting a kink in my neck, though. I wasn't exactly a tall woman.

They lived down the road from me in a small trailer with their mother and an older sister. We had less than five residents on Farm Market Road, and I lived in the only brick house. The rest of the residences were single or double wide trailers in really good condition. Just passing by, one would never be able to even guess they were trailers.

"Hi Julio," I said, then turned to Hector. "Hello. What can I do for you guys?"

The boys' eyes went from my bare feet all the way up to my unkempt hair. Normally, I carried myself well. I always wore my black hair pulled up, in a shiny and professional manner. Except today.

"Our mom wanted to know if you wanted to buy Tamales today," Julio told me.

"Not today, Julio. Thank you very much for asking." What was the point of buying food? I wouldn't be around to eat it once they left. "Tell Ms. Ana that I say thank you for everything." The Ramirez family was always so nice to me, and such an amazingly beautiful family. I always admired how Ms. Ana pushed on, especially after her husband left to go back to Mexico.

"Okay," Julio replied, dragging his brother away.

"Life is not fair." Hector's whisper brushed against my ear, but I almost couldn't understand what he had said. Then, he continued, a little louder. "I can't get a BB gun and the crazy Cat Lady walks around with a forty-five."

When did I became the Cat Lady?

"What would you do for one?" I asked Hector. It took everything in me not to slap a hand over my mouth. I had no clue what had come over me. The words had just oozed out of me.

The boys went stiff, eyeing me with open-mouthed stares. "Lady, I ain't doing no kinky shit for a gun," Hector shot out.

I was afraid to ask what he meant by "kinky." All I wanted was to get the grass mowed before my funeral.

"Hector, let's go." Julio dragged his brother away before I could say another word.

I threw the door from my hand and kicked it shut, which wasn't a great idea with no shoes on. Sucking in a breath at my now stubbed toe, I moved towards the couch. I'd reached a new level of embarrassment. I was the town's Cat Lady. Every town had one, and I was this towns. I shook my head and ran a hand through my wild hair. I needed to get this done soon.

Beep, beep. What in Jesus was that? I searched the living room, finding the culprit of the sound underneath some magazines and books on my coffee table.

Nobody ever comes to my house or calls, but today *everyone* wants to make an appearance.

"God, if you are trying to tell me something, why don't you just send me an email." Oh, probably because I haven't check those in over a month.

Beep, beep. The stupid phone wasn't stopping.

I grabbed it with my free hand and checked the caller ID. Lord help me, it was Mother. If I didn't answer, she would either keep calling or she'd come over. Might as well get this over with.

With a sigh, I slid the answer button across the screen. "Yes, Mother?" I said as sweetly as possible.

"What took you so long?" Barbara Carter was a force to be reckoned with—a southern lady to the core. Even in her seventies, she was fashionable, elegant, and always to the point. "I know you don't have anything else going on."

"The Ramirez boys were at the door," I told her, sticking to a safe topic.

"Did you order tamales?" she asked quickly.

"Not today, Mother." I didn't need to explain why.

"That's a shame, but also a good thing. We are having lunch at the senior center, so come and join us." Mother's tone left no room for argument.

"Mother, I got laundry to do." I needed to at least.

"Angela, you have all day to get laundry done," Mother replied in her most authoritarian tone, which translated to me being in trouble. "Get over here as quickly as possible."

Before I could argue, she hung up. That woman always had to have the last word. I was forty-five years old. I didn't have to be afraid of Mother any more. I could stay home if I wanted to. But I was planning to end my life. Did I really want Mother's last memory of me to be this conversation? Even now, so close to my end, I was trying to make things easier for everyone else.

Guess I'm going out to lunch now, I thought with a frown.

I placed the gun on the table and headed to my room to change. Bringing guns to the center was not a problem. We lived in Texas, after all. However, leaving it home was the surest way my mother wouldn't get her hands on it. And if her crazy group of friends saw it...I'd be doomed. All of them owned a revolver and 9mm, but they always wanted more.

Father, give me the strength to make it through this lunch, I prayed to myself as I considered what clothes to wear.

Chapter Two

$\mathcal{I}$ made it to the Senior Center in less than fifteen minutes. Sunshine was tiny, located in the middle of Cass County. The place was so small it didn't even have a traffic light. In fact, most of us were excited when the city decided to put one of those flashing yellow lights at the main intersection. With one Texas Highway that passed through our town, traffic could get a little messy. Unfortunately, we still weren't big enough for a Walmart.

The Senior Center was located right on Main Street. It was near the general store with the only gas station in town, the Baptist Church, and the main cemetery. We had more seniors, or soon to be seniors, in town than any other group. Sunshine had somehow become the county's retirement community. The senior center was the largest building and the most modern. It had also become the community center.

The parking lot was full, but I found one empty spot on the far right side. The summer heat had finally dimmed, a blessing if ever there was one. Fall was usually a short season here, and for the most part, winters were mild. In fact, colder days were virtually nonexistent until January or February, and even then, they didn't last long.

I wore a long dress with my hair pulled tight in a bun, which was perfect for the weather. I would like to say I got dressed up, but this was my normal look.

Wandering eyes landed on me, so I ran inside to avoid all the people gossiping, but that mission failed miserably when Mother said, "Hi, Angela." I stopped in my tracks and nodded in greeting.

Mother and her ladies sat at an table opposite the entrance, which forced me to say hi to most of the people in the hall.

I waved politely and avoided small talk. I knew I was violating all the cardinal rules in the south, but I just wanted to get to the table and hide. However, even when I sat down in the empty chair, I could still hear the murmurs about me.

Minnie waved at me from the table. Mother was the youngest out of her friends, and that was saying a lot since she was in her seventies. Minnie was the oldest in her early eighties, and she still wore her bright red lipstick that brought out her shiny white hair.

Next to her were Ethel and Florence. They were in their seventies and sisters. They were also out of control. Ethel refused to be defined as traditional and would only wear slacks and cardigans. If the feminist movement needed a leader, Ethel would be their first choice. Florence, on the other hand, was stuck in the fifties and still believed she was a pin-up girl. Somehow, she managed to dress in that fashion and make it look good. I envied her courage so much more than I had ever said out loud.

"Hi there, ladies. Thank you for saving me a seat," I told the group as I sat down on the empty chair.

"What took you so long?" Mother asked, the words rushing out of her.

"I had to get dressed," I told her, not making eye contact.

"And that's what you picked?" Mother eyed my clothes. "Angela, you look like something a coyote dragged across the woods. And why are you not wearing any make up? What happened to your hair?"

"Angie, dear, have you been eating?" Florence asked me, trying to turn the conversation away from Mother's attacks. "You are shrinking into nothing. Honey, ribs are not sexy." She inspected me with a careful look. I didn't know what was more traumatizing: having a seventy-year-old woman telling me what wasn't sexy, or the fact that she was doing it in public.

"What my sister means to say is you do not appear healthy," Ethel jumped in.

"That is true. You don't look healthy, but you definitely don't look sexy, either." Florence crossed her arms over her chest. Old people were great, with their nonexistent filters and all. It was amazing that they could say whatever they wanted, no matter if it was the most embarrassing thing in the world or not. "Angie, have you ever seen those commercials on TV about those starving kids and thought, 'Man, that is one sexy look?' No! Nobody does. Because protruding bones are not sexy."

I dropped my head on the table and prayed the floor would

swallow me whole.

"Honey, you aren't still yearning over that two-timing loser, are you?" Minnie asked with her hand on my shoulder.

"Of course not." I lifted my head but looked at the table, because if I looked up, they would know I'd lied.

"Angela, you are a terrible liar," Mother added. "It's been nine months since your divorce. You cannot continue to hide away in your house." She glared at me as she spoke.

"I'm sorry." The words came out louder than I had intended, which had people turning and watching me. I counted to ten. In a lower tone, I continued. "Sorry, it's taken me a while to get over twenty-seven years of marriage." I closed my eyes to hold back the tears that threatened to spill, just like they always did any time I tried to talk about *him*.

"You were miserable most of the time," Ethel jumped in. "Sometimes you can do better on your own."

Easy for her to say, she had never been married.

"I'm just glad your father is not here to see this," Mother said and for once, I agreed with her. "Because he would have killed Todd by now. He drained your inheritance, let us support him for years, and now he leaves you." It looked like Mother's face might explode at any minute. It just kept getting redder and redder with each tick of the clock.

"Angie, why don't you go get some food?" Minnie said, saving me from the rest of the lecture. "Joyce is catering today."

"Minnie, you make it sound like Joyce doesn't cater our events *every* day." Ethel shook her head.

The ladies were vicious today. What had gotten them more fired up than they usually were?

"It's chicken spaghetti. You know it's going to be good." Minnie gave me a shove and pushed me out of the chair.

I made my way slowly towards the kitchen, staring down at the floor to avoid making eye contact with everyone. It had been a great plan, until I bumped into someone because I couldn't see my surroundings.

"I'm sorry," I mumbled as I looked into the most gorgeous pair of brown eyes I'd seen in a long time.

It took me a minute to recognize him as James Brooks, the county judge. James stood at about six-two and was still in great shape for a man entering his fifties, but next to him, I felt short. He also still had a full head of brown hair.

"Oh no, it's my fault for stopping in the middle of the walkway. How are you, Angela?" James's eyes sparkled like a kid up to some mischief when he spoke.

"I'm good, thank you," I said in a soft voice, praying he hadn't heard the conversation at our table.

"I heard about your divorce. I'm sorry," James said, and a sadness passed over his features. James was a widower and the most eligible bachelor in the county. The last thing I needed was his pity.

"Life must be very slow in Liden if my divorce made it all the way to the county seat," I said, trying to play it off to keep my dignity intact.

"I make it a point to keep up with cases in my county," James said. "But I'm sorry. If you ever need to talk, I'm here. I know how hard it is to lose someone after being together for so long. Divorce is still a loss." He lowered his voice so only I could hear it.

"Thank you," I mumbled as quickly as I could and waved good bye. It was a good thing I was ending it all today. My self-esteem couldn't handle anymore destruction.

I finally made it to the serving area. The struggle to get there was almost nonexistent, probably a blessing from being late. Ms. Joyce and her team had prepared a feast for an army. My mouth watered as soon as the smells wafted around me, making me realize it had been a few days since I actually had a proper meal, so I grabbed a plate, only to be stopped by Ms. Joyce.

"Angela dear, are you okay?" Ms. Joyce leaned in and asked me in a quiet voice. Even with her getting closer, I still had to look up to meet her eyes since she was taller than me by at least four inches.

Ms. Joyce was a legend in our town. She was the first black woman to start a business back when segregation was only something talked about and not practiced. She was fearless. The sheer power of her conviction and determination broke every barrier that anyone tried to put in front of her. *No* was not an answer she ever accepted. It was no wonder Ms. Joyce and Mother had become good friends. Their personalities alone could set the rainforest on fire. When the two of them got together, it was hard to tell which one was the flame and which one the gas; they just fed off each other.

"I'm fine," I replied softly.

"I know you aren't, but I won't push. Here, this is for your kids." Ms. Joyce gave me a small goodie bag for the kids, then handed me a large plate of food for me. "Tuna salad and an extra piece of pecan pie for you." She squeezed my hand and her touch was gentle. "Honey, I know you are hurting, but the first step to recovery is to forgive."

"Please, not you too. I've heard that a million times already. Forgive and forget." My voice cracked as I worked hard to hold back the tears.

"Who said anything about forgetting? Don't you ever forget!" Ms. Joyce's voice was sharp and a deep frown lined her face. "You forgive the wrong that was done to you. Forgive yourself so you don't carry the guilt and shame with you. Then, when you are ready, you make them all pay. Do you hear me?" She stared hard at me, almost like she was trying to read my soul. And I had a feeling she could.

"Make them pay?" I barely uttered the words.

"There will be a day of reckoning. In the meantime, you show that asshole and that Barbie Doll of his who is really in charge." Because I hardly ever curse, hearing Ms. Joyce do it caused a heat to creep into my cheeks.

"You nicknamed her Barbie Doll?" I asked, surprise apparent in the high-pitched tone of my voice.

"Honey, there is nothing real about that girl," she told me as she looked around the room. "She's bleached blonde, has fake boobs, and butt implants. Barbie has more original parts than she does." She laughed at her own joke and I joined in.

"This too shall pass, right?" I asked after my laugher stopped.

"Only if you let it," Ms. Joyce replied and patted my cheeks.

I headed back to the table with my "kitty" bag and plate of food. The ladies were all in deep conversation, which made me afraid to ask what they were talking about.

"What were you talking about with James Brooks?" Mother asked, a little too giddy for my taste.

"Nothing, really. The food," I replied as I started eating.

"That is one good looking man," Florence added from her side of the table. "If I was twenty years younger, I'd be all over that. You should go for him, Angela." The minute those last words passed her lips, I choked, which had Minnie and Mother patting my back to save me. From death or embarrassment, I wasn't sure, though.

"I'm good," I finally said when my breathing returned to

normal. "I'll pass on that. I don't need another lawyer in my life. Remember how the last one turned out," I told the ladies as I lost my appetite. "I think it's time for me to head home."

"But you just got here, and you haven't even finished your food yet," Ethel said with big puppy eyes.

"I know, but I forgot to feed the cats and Ms. Joyce just gave me food for them." I got up as quickly as possible and pulled my goodie bag with me. "Have a great time everyone." I waved at the ladies. "I love you Mother," I told her as I leaned down and kissed her cheek.

"Angela, are you okay?" Mother asked, trying to get up from her chair.

"I'm fine," I said, but I knew she would see right through my lie, so I turned and almost ran out of the hall. I had to make sure her last memory of me was a good one, which made me a little glad that she'd called today.

I got to my car as quickly as I could, not giving anyone the chance to stop me. The car was an old, beat-down Honda that I hated. Todd took the Lexus in the divorce, claiming I wouldn't be able to afford it. He never mentioned the down payment for that thing came from my bank account.

Tears had turned to a steady stream rolling down my face by the time I pulled away from the parking lot. It made anger course through me. I never wanted to cry another tear for that man.

Chapter Three

*A*s I marched in to my living room, I realized how much I hated everything. The bright yellow walls taunted me with their cheerfulness. Mother had given Todd and me the house not long after Dad died. Before that, we had lived in one of her rental houses not too far from this place. According to her, the house was too big for her. How sad was it that I'd never lived anywhere but here my entire life? I didn't even go away to college, choosing instead to marry right after high school. It wasn't until recently that I ever regretted both of those decisions.

I paced the room, forcing the tears to stay away. It wouldn't be long now. I didn't even bother changing back to my house clothes. If I did it right, the blood and brain matter wouldn't destroy the dress. Clyde and Bonnie slowly sauntered out of the main bedroom. I hated that stupid room. I hadn't slept in that bed since he'd left, but I also didn't have the nerve to sell it. What would people think if I did?

The bathroom, on the other hand, would be the better choice. I could pick either one of them. The clean-up would be much easier then. Hopefully my death wouldn't destroy the value of the house too much.

Getting lost in my thoughts kept delaying me. It was now or never. I grabbed the Smith and Wesson and made my way toward the guest bathroom. Since it was right off the living room, I wouldn't have to see the bed I hated so much before I died.

Ring.

I stopped in the middle of the room and stared at the front door. This had to be a joke. Nobody ever visited me.

I let out a long breath and looked at the walls as I made my way to the door. What had I been thinking when I painted this room yellow? With a sigh, I yanked the door open to find Julio and Hector back on my threshold.

"Was Ms. Ana not able to sell all the tamales?" I asked the boys.

"Mom sold everything early today," Julio said, shoving his hands in his pockets and kicking imaginary rocks around while he avoided making any kind of eye contact with me.

"Did you mean it?" Hector blurted out, checking the street up and down as he readjusted his hood.

"What are you talking about?" I asked the boys, folding my arms over my chest and not the least bit concerned that the movement put my gun on full display.

"About the gun," Hector replied, pointing to the Smith and Wesson with his chin.

"I was under the impression you weren't planning to do any freaky shit for a gun," I told Hector with a mocking smile.

It amazed me that because I knew I would shortly die I could be as cocky and arrogant as I'd always wanted but never managed. And obviously my statement had taken the boys by surprise as well, at least if their wide opened-mouth stares were any indication.

"Oh children, please," I said, shaking my head. "I was thinking of you cutting my grass. Other than chores, I have no use for little boys in my life. Good bye." I uncrossed my arms and grabbed the door handle, shoving it closed.

But it didn't close. Julio stopped it with his palm. "Wait. It's not for us." That made me halt.

I half turned back toward him. "Who is it for?" My words came out slow as my gaze roamed the street, just like poor Hector had done earlier.

"For me." A tall young man stepped around my flower beds, towering behind the boys.

He was probably in his early twenties, around six feet tall with a mocha complexion, dark black eyes, and some weird dye job in his hair, making the tips look like they were frosted in gold. Hector and Julio looked a lot more wholesome—well, maybe not Hector. He looked mischievous, but that wasn't necessarily a bad thing.

The new guy, though, radiated danger as his eyes scanned me up and down in a predatory way. I had seen Clyde do the same once when he was hunting mice.

"And who are you supposed to be?" I asked frosty, throwing

my manners to the wind.

"Maybe we should continue this conversation inside. What would the neighbors think of you entertaining young men at your door," Frosty told me, pointing to the trailer across the street.

He had a point. The trailer was owned by Dolores, the town's gossip queen.

"Strangers don't come in my house," I said, meaning it. In less than ten minutes, I would kill myself, so nosy neighbors were the least of my concern in that moment.

"Tony," he said, but that was all he gave me.

Who did the guy think he was? Cher?

"No last name?" I asked as I inched outside and closed the door.

"None that you would recognize," Tony answered, crossing his arms over his chest.

What *Tony* didn't realize was the war he was fighting was one he couldn't win. I wouldn't be backing down anytime soon. What did I have to lose? Absolutely nothing,

"Try me," I replied.

"Berrido. My family comes from the Caribbean." I had a feeling Tony added the last part as a goodwill act.

"Unique," I told the young man who carried himself with a certain level of charisma that was normally reserved for older gentlemen. "Now that I know you, you're no longer a stranger, so come in," I told him, opening the door again.

Tony crossed the threshold with the grace of a cat. "I am assuming you two are joining him, right?" I asked the twins.

"Of course," Hector replied, trying to imitate Tony, although he failed miserably. His head might've been held high, but his lower lip quivered, ruining the effect.

"Ms. Angela, I'm so sorry," Julio whispered. "I won't let anything happen to you." The last part he said even softer as he followed behind the other two. This was getting stranger by the minute.

I closed the door and slowly made my way to the living room. I took my time, rearranging photos on the wall as I went. The living room was classically arranged, with a sofa, a love seat, and a recliner, and all of those things surrounded the black wooden table in the center. The table was my act of defiance against Mother. She had hated that table, calling it "too modern."

Tony took the recliner and sat like a king with his legs crossed. The twins took a seat on the sofa, leaving a full space between them, and Julio had taken the seat closest to where I was about to sit. I guessed he was really taking his mission to protect me seriously. I should've told him he didn't need to. Not with what I was about to do.

I took a seat on the right side of the love seat and made a big show of fixing my dress. After rearranging my skirt several times, I placed the Smith and Wesson on the table in front of me. Very slowly and almost ceremoniously, I placed my hands on my lap and sat up straight. This was still my house and I was a southern lady after all. A broke southern lady, but still a lady, nevertheless.

"Gentlemen, I don't have all day, so please get to your business," I said, making sure my accent was thick. For some strange reason, people assumed a person couldn't be as smart as them if they had an accent. Unless it was a European one, or course.

"Hector said you were interested in selling your gun," Tony said.

"I might have mentioned something like that. Why do you care?" I asked the little trickster sitting across from me.

I was married to a lying, cunning lawyer for twenty-seven years, so this poor kid had no chance at deceiving me today.

"I'm in the market for some weapons, and I would like to purchase yours," Tony explained, leaning forward in his chair.

I had to blink several times because I was sure he was batting his eyelashes at me. Was he trying to flirt with me? This boy was in desperate need of therapy.

"That could be a possibility," I told Tony turned Romeo, knowing perfectly well I wasn't going to sell this gun. This was my weapon of choice.

"You wouldn't happen to have any more?" Tony asked in a soft purr. By the sensual way he caressed my recliner, I was sure the boy had experience with the ladies.

"I might," I answered, sitting up taller in my seat. I wasn't a prude, maybe not much, but I couldn't let this boy know how uncomfortable he made me.

"I would like to make a business deal," Tony said, that soft purr of his coming even thicker.

"What if I'm not interested in a deal with you?" I asked him.

A wicked smile spread across his face. With a flick of his

wrists, he had a beautiful Ruger LC380 out. Unfortunately, he held that baby like most thugs on TV do, one handed and with a strange sideways tilt.

"Ms. Angela, we don't want this to turn ugly," Tony replied without a hint of playfulness in his voice.

It was my turn to smile back. I slowly fixed the skirt of my dress and slid my hands to the cracks of the love seat. Something snapped in me. I was okay with killing myself, but the idea of someone else doing it for me made me furious inside. Two could play this game, and I pulled a 9mm out and pointed it at Tony.

"Oh, I'm pretty sure it will get ugly, but mostly for you," I told Tony with the sweetest and fakest Sunday church smile I could muster. I had years of practice holding my tongue and smiling when I really wanted to scream. This little situation was no different.

"Well it seems it's a good thing I didn't bring a knife to a gun fight," Tony said, leaning back in the recliner.

"That would have been disappointing," I replied, picking the imaginary lint off my skirt.

"How do you know I won't just shoot you and take everything?" Tony asked, pointing at my weapons with his gun.

"You won't," I said with the same fake smile. I eyed the twins, noticing they had turned a different shade of green.

Interesting. I have never seen anyone that color brown change to green, I thought.

"What makes you so sure?" Tony asked, ignoring the boys.

"Simple, little boy," I said, relaxing into the corner of the love seat. "That little baby you're carrying has way more recoil than you could possibly handle with one hand. If you're lucky, you'll blow a hole in my chandelier and maybe bust your knee cap." I gave the chandelier a brief look. That would be a blessing for me, actually. The thing was pretentious and hideous. I couldn't believe I let my ex buy it, let alone actually install it.

The twins' eyes were on the chandelier when I glanced back at Tony. "What's much more likely to happen is you will shoot Hector, then I'll be forced to put two rounds in your chest before you kill Julio, too." I delivered my prediction with a wink and started tapping my foot.

"What?" screamed Hector.

"This is Texas, dear, and you are trespassing. Castle Law, nobody would ever doubt that a sweet, lonely cat lady had to shoot an intruder to defend herself," I told Tony as I rearranged my skirt again.

"God save us," Julio prayed.

"Are you ready to die, dear?" I asked Hector, who looked clammy and had started shaking everywhere. "I have made my peace with the devil, how about you Tony?" I turned my demented smile on Tony. I wasn't sure how crazy I sounded, but Tony's lower lip looked like it was trembling. I guessed he wasn't nearly as tough as he thought he was.

"Aghhh!" Tony screamed as Clyde somersaulted from who knew where and landed directly on his lap.

I didn't waste any time and crossed the space between us. By the time I reached him, Bonnie had jumped on his head. Before the boy could move, I'd taken his gun away.

"Good job, Clyde. That's my girl, Bonnie." I praised my little kiddies as I made my way back to my side of the room. "Please leave him now." Clyde growled at Tony but slowly climbed down. He dug his claws in as he descended down his legs, but I was pretty sure he'd gotten his private parts too.

"Oh God!" Tony screamed, trying to pull away. He couldn't, though. Not with Bonnie wrapped around his neck the way she was.

"Bonnie, now." I really had no clue if that would work. Usually my cats weren't ones to follow instructions very well, but good old Bonnie bit the tip of Tony's ear just as I'd hoped, making him bounce off the recliner.

"What the fuck? Who are you?" Tony was trying to get up when both Bonnie and Clyde jumped on the living room table and stared him down. I wasn't a gambling woman, but my money was on the cats. "How are you controlling them? What are you, a possessed cat lady or something?"

"I wish," I told him as I got comfortable in my love seat again. "If I had that power, I would be a widow and not a lonely divorcée." Julio laughed at my joke while Hector eyed the cats with a weary look. "They just happen to be a little overprotective, that's all."

"Are they going to attack me again?" Tony asked, his eyes never leaving the cats.

"That's up to you. Don't do anything stupid and they will leave you alone," I told Tony. After my words, he relaxed back into his chair.

Bonnie and Clyde followed suit and slowly lowered themselves on the table. If the guys in this room hadn't known any better, they'd probably believe they were just normal, sweet house cats.

"Are you ready to talk business or just threaten a helpless cat lady?" I asked Tony, my voice like silk running down a spine.

"Hell lady, there is nothing helpless about you," Tony told me. His eyes looked me up and down, kind of as if he was seeing me for the first time.

"Don't be so dramatic, child." My eyes went to his Ruger. "Now, tell me what you need?"

"War is coming, and my people need protection," Tony said, and he now had my undivided attention. I placed both guns on my lap and leaned forward.

"War is coming to Texas?" If that was the case, I might need the guns myself.

"Not yet, but its right over the border, closer than anyone realizes," Tony told me. "People are disappearing and even the cartels are running scared. I'm in charge of the border and we are low on guns and ammo. Can you help?" The flirting little boy had exited the building, and in his place was a man who was so nervous about what was coming that he kept running his hands through his hair.

"Let me think about it. Come back tomorrow and you'll have your answer," I told him.

"Tomorrow?" Tony's eyes fell to the twins for support, but they were too busy examining Bonnie and Clyde to give him any.

"The real question is, can you pay for them?" I asked, a little curious.

"We can make it worth your time," Tony replied.

"In the Immortal words of Hector, I'm not doing any freaky shit here," I told Tony, tilting my head.

Tony's melodious laugh filled the room. "You are funny lady; I like you. No freaky shit, just plain old Benjamins." He stood from his seat and smiled at me.

I climbed to my feet, holding both guns.

"Can I get my gun back?" Tony asked, extending his hand toward me.

"When you learn how to hold it, you can have it back," I told him.

"Fair enough," Tony answered. "Would you mind at least considering a discount for a group of underground fighters?"

I rolled my eyes. "Come back tomorrow and I might give you the Cat Lady Special. Good bye, Tony," I said, dismissing him.

"Good bye, Ms. Angela," Tony said

I escorted the boys to the door in silence, then watched as they headed in opposite directions. After they disappeared from view, I closed the door and headed back to the living room, dropping the two new guns next to my Smith right before I sat on the love seat again.

"Well guys, guess we are not dying tonight," I told the cats.

"MEOW!!!" both cats screamed back, their fur standing up on all ends like they'd been struck by a massive jolt of static electricity.

"Fine, you are not dying, period." Their fur relaxed at my words. "Am I really going to sell arms to kids?" I asked the cats as I leaned down on the sofa, reaching over my head to pull the blanket I kept over the back down on me.

"What do I got to lose?" I asked them.

"Meow," Clyde replied.

"I don't have any skills that would translate to the workforce in this new world. I can't grow marijuana, and there is no way I could make meth. I'm too proud, and probably too lousy, to sell sex. But thanks to my good old dad, I know about guns." I looked at Bonnie and Clyde for moral support. "Should we do this, guys?"

I had no idea why I was debating life and death decisions with cats, but I had nobody else. Bonnie and Clyde jumped across the table and landed on me, knocking the air out of my lungs. Bonnie licked my face with her sandpaper tongue and Clyde rubbed his head under my neck.

"Seriously? We are doing this?" I asked my cats again.

"Meow," they both replied again.

"Okay. I guess the worst-case scenario is that this goes bad and we are back to plan A."

Both cats stared at me and started purring.

"Arms dealer it is." I made myself comfortable and let my kids lull me to sleep.

Chapter Four

I couldn't sleep all night. This crazy idea of being an arms dealer wouldn't leave my mind. It was nuts, demented even. If I sold guns to these young boys so they could smuggle them across the border, could I live with myself? I tossed around as I laid on the couch, and Bonnie and Clyde looked down at me from their favorite perch on top of the sofa.

I let out a long sigh. In less than a week, my childhood home would be gone. I'd be on the streets with nowhere to go when it happened. I had given up everything to support my husband, to boost his career. I'd even been doing it the day he walked out.

Yeah, my pride had taken a kick, and in some ways, so had my morals.

I rolled off the sofa at dawn, still as awake as the moment I had laid down to begin with. It wouldn't matter how long I laid there. It wasn't bringing me any closer to any answers, so I climbed to my feet and moved through the quiet house. The hardwood floor ran the length of the house, until the kitchen where we—no, wait, where *I* had placed every tile down. Todd couldn't be disturbed to help with that project, or any other for that matter.

The cold tiles attacked my bare feet as I made my way across the kitchen. I needed coffee. Bad. Maybe an IV of it would bring my brain back to life and make my body function. The cats' automated feeder went off, and all I saw was fur flying by. That had to have been the best purchase I'd ever made.

With the kids busy, I pressed the button in the coffee maker and waited. Luckily, I'd filled everything the night before just to save time.

The aroma of coffee filled the kitchen and relaxed my nerves. I couldn't wait for that first sip, the one that always tasted like paradise. It was too late to save my soul from my coffee addiction.

And this could be the beginning of it. First coffee, next cocaine.

My daydream of self-destruction was cut short when I saw yesterday's paper. I hadn't paid that much attention when I'd glanced at it the previous day, but now I couldn't look away from the headlines.

Todd was getting married.

Raged filled my soul like a thousand angry bees with their stingers at the ready. I ripped the paper to shreds. Screams filled the air, and it took a minute to realize it was me screaming. Of course it was. I happened to be the only person in the room. Before I could stop myself, I picked up a wooden spoon from the counter and flung it at the wall, then I hurled some onion soup packets. Next, I kicked the wall like Todd's impending marriage was its fault.

Stupid mint wall. Why did I paint this kitchen mint?

Thirty minutes later, I was on the floor in the kitchen covered in newspaper shreds and broken dishes. The kids sat above me, putting a safe distance between them and me. Their big eyes stared down at me with what looked like sadness.

What in the hell was wrong with me? Laying on the floor covered in a broken mess of my possessions like a shattered person. Todd believed I was nothing without him. That self-centered, sorry excuse of a lawyer thought he made me better. I couldn't let him know he'd won, and if he came back right now, there would be no doubt in his mind that he had.

With a renewed sense of determination, I wiped the snot from my face, dried my tears, and shook off the dirt from my clothes.

"We are doing this kids," I announced to the cats. "I don't need a man to save me." Drained of emotions, I mustered the little dignity I had left and forced myself to get up from the floor.

"Meow," sweet little Bonnie said.

"I'm good sweetie," I lied to her. Fake it until you make it would be my new mantra, at least until I found myself again. Who knew how long that would take?

Clyde stood by the coffee maker as I made my way toward him. When I pulled out a coffee mug, he climbed inside the cabinet, probably eyeing his kiddy treats.

"Meow!" Clyde screamed in a high pitch.

I reached into the cabinet in the same direction that Clyde had gone. My head pounded from all the crying, but I knew how happy my kiddies would be if I gave them a treat. Only, Clyde wasn't after a treat. Instead, he pushed over an unopened bottle of Irish Cream Mother had given me.

Was I imagining this? My eyes buried into my cat, but he was definitely winning the staring contest.

"What the heck? I'll need courage today if we are doing this," I told Clyde as I pulled the bottle out and poured a healthy dose in my mug. Brown liquid followed the cream, and when I took my first sip, my eyes rolled back in my head at the heavenly taste.

"It's five o'clock somewhere," I told Clyde.

"Meow," he replied.

"You are a bad influence, my friend, but cheers." I raised my mug and for a second, I thought my cat was smiling back at me. This was going to be a wild day. I took another large gulp and steadied myself. "I need to get ready and stop by the bunker. I forgot to ask what time they were coming."

For an arms dealer, I really needed to work on specific instructions. Stop by tomorrow was not the best way to set up a meeting.

I made my way quickly to the master bedroom. My clothes were still in the walk-in closet in the bathroom, which was attached to the master bedroom. I loved that bathroom, especially since Todd hated it after I'd renovated. Maybe it was my subconscious way of rebelling against all his rules and demands.

I rushed inside and set out clothes as the water warmed up. As I glanced at my closet, I realized I didn't have any pants. Todd had hated pants on women. I shook my head, realizing I should have never let him control me.

After I took a quick shower, I dressed even faster, ready to start my new venture, but memories threatened to consume me. I rushed out to the backyard through the patio with my hair still wet. The soft morning light of October kind of took my breath away as I glanced out across the three acres I owned. In Texas standard, it wasn't too impressive, but for a single, suicidal woman, it was a pain in the rear to keep up.

My dad had put a fence up for protection before he'd passed, and at the far end of the property he'd built a small shed. According to Mother, the shed was my dad's hiding spot to play with all his toys, although my poor mother had no clue what he'd been playing with back there.

Out of habit, I looked around to make sure nobody had their eyes on me. It was crazy. I knew nobody was ever in my backyard, but it didn't stop me from inspecting the area. Maybe I had finally become as paranoid as my dad.

I entered the shed and turned on the light. The riding lawnmower was neatly parked on one side. Tools lined one whole wall of the shed. There were no windows, so I locked the door with my key.

This stupid key was my dad's dying gift. He made me promise never to let Todd inside. I knew my dad never liked Todd, but at the time, I'd thought this had been a bit excessive. Lucky for me, Todd believed he was a city dweller and never wanted to set foot outside the house. If he only knew.

I made my way to the far corner and pushed aside a toolbox to expose the trapdoor underneath. I found it by accident the day I'd decided to cut the apple tree down—the one I'd planted for Todd out of love. Maybe I should've been grateful. I would've never found this if it hadn't been for his betrayal.

I pulled the trap door open and unlocked the second set of doors that led down to my dad's bunker. It shouldn't have surprised me. I'd always known my dad had built a bunker, just like so many other people in Texas. Nobody could say we wouldn't be prepared for the Apocalypse.

What I hadn't been prepared for was the thousands of weapons and ammo my dad had stored in that bunker. It was at least thirty by forty feet and almost two stories deep. This place had shelving, bookcases, lock boxes, and even display stands. This was a militia's wet dream. It had been six months since I found this place and I still hadn't inventoried the whole thing.

This morning I was short on time, though, so I rushed to a corner of the bunker where all the 9mms were located. I wanted something compact that could be easily concealed. Dad was a pro when it came to weapons. His collection of handguns was impressive.

With the little amount of information flirt boy had given me, I decided on five Ruger LC9s and five Taurus 709s. If Tony liked his Ruger, then the least I could do was help supply some.

However, I needed something to carry this all outside.

"Thank you, Dad," I whispered when I found two beautiful briefcases. Dad had always thought of everything.

I set the cases on the table and loaded the guns. They were in pristine condition, but I still wanted to clean them before the boys showed up. I had cleaning rags and oils stored in my garage, and that meant I could move this little project to my patio while I waited. I was all about comfort.

Chapter Five

It was close to noon when I heard the bell at the back gate go off. The only good investment that ex of mine made me get had been a state-of-the-art security system. Granted, now I knew he'd only added it so he would know when I was home or not. Still, it allowed me to hear the gates and doors being opened from anywhere in the house.

The house had a beautiful screened-in patio that was currently very neglected. Normally, by this time of the year, my potted plants were inside my garage, leaving the place pristine for winter. Today I had dead leaves everywhere, the patio furniture was filthy, and bugs littered the ground. This place was a disgrace for a well-raised woman, but considering the house was on the chopping block to get repossessed, good housekeeping hadn't been my top priority.

Truthfully, at this moment in my life, I couldn't find the energy to care. Not when I'd been cleaning guns all morning, which made me giddy with joy. My mood was lighter than it had been in months. Guns were something I understood and felt secure around.

Julio and Hector came down the paved sidewalk that surrounded my house. The weather was mild, so it surprised me to see the boys wearing hoodies.

"Hi Ms. Angela. We heard your music. Hope you don't mind that we came this way," Julio said, offering a wave in greeting.

"Hi Julio. Hello Hector," I told the boys and lowered the music in my old CD player. I had a feeling I might be one of the last few people on the planet that still had one. When I glanced at the boys again, they stood on the outside of the patio. "What's going on?"

"Mami told us to come apologize to you and ask if you want us to cancel this whole deal with Tony." Julio and Hector had their heads down and their hands shoved deep into their pockets.

"As long as your friend doesn't try to kill me, we are doing this," I told the boys. Both of their heads snapped up at those words, and their eyes went wide. I raised my eyebrows at them. "Yes, that's right. I'm doing this, so stop your staring already. You both know that's rude. Get in here."

Both boys rushed through the door. Hector made it to the table first, while Julio kept a bit of distance and stood behind him.

"Touch one of them and you will be missing a finger," I told Hector as he reached for one of the guns. "I'm not planning another half an hour cleaning session because of smudgy finger prints." I grinned because I knew I wouldn't really mind doing it all over again.

"Tony called," Hector finally spoke. "He wants to come over in fifteen to see the merchandise and make the deal." His hands went back in his pockets and he bounced back and forth on the balls of his feet.

"In that case, call him back and tell him to come now," I told him, pointing at the guns. "I'm as ready as I'm going to be."

Hector's eyes lit up with excitement. "Yes ma'am." He stepped away from the patio to make the call. Julio's eyes were on his brother as he ran off, and the minute he was alone he paced the length of the patio.

"Julio, what's wrong?" I asked him, placing the guns back in their case. I'd chosen to wear soft, cotton gloves to avoid finger prints, but they were starting to make my hands sweat.

"Nothing," he muttered.

"You just like to make trenches in my patio for the sake of it?" I asked him with my eyebrows raised.

"We are really sorry, Ms. Angela," Julio told me with teary eyes. "Mami said this was really dangerous and could get you killed. I was only trying to help." He shoved his hands in his pockets, resembling his brother in that moment.

"Help me how?" I asked.

"We heard you were going to lose the house and we thought you could use the money." Julio threw the words at me in a rush. "Money is hard to come by for everyone, but we don't want you to get hurt."

A smile filled my heart. Julio was a good kid, even if his wild brother tried to drag him into all sorts of crazy adventures.

"I guess everyone knows," I said, letting out a long breath. Julio just nodded. "Times are tough, sure, but that doesn't mean we are going to die. There could be an old-fashioned gun fight, but I guarantee we won't be dying." I winked at him.

We heard the bell go off. Julio and I turned towards the gate and waited until Hector waltzed in with Tony in tow.

"I didn't think you had time to make a call yet," I told both boys in place of a greeting.

"Tony was waiting outside for me," Hector said, stepping back into the patio room.

"Morning Ms. Angela," Tony said, tipping his cowboy hat towards me. If you didn't know him, he looked like a good-ol-country boy with a great tan. The hat did an impressive job at hiding those weird frosted tips.

"Good morning, Tony," I replied, standing up to be as close to eye level as possible. Tony was at least six feet, so it was definitely a challenge.

"What do you have for me?" Tony asked, walking towards the patio table that had become my work station.

I turned the cases in his direction to give him a better view of the guns. Julio moved behind me, almost like a bodyguard. Hector took a position near the door and kept his eyes on Tony. The boys definitely didn't trust the guy.

Tony leaned down to inspect the guns, holding his arms out to his sides. "May I?"

"Of course. Just remember to wipe down any that you touch. Fingerprints need to be removed before delivery," I told him in a calm voice.

I should be scared. This whole thing could go seriously wrong. But for some strange reason, a tranquil feeling had settled over me, along with a sense of excitement. Maybe I'd made my peace with death, so living on the wild side no longer scared me. Maybe I'd just lost my marbles and had gone crazy. Whatever it was, it made me feel free and I kind of liked that.

Tony pulled out a Taurus and examined the gun. It seemed like he knew what to look for, even though he held the gun like an idiot.

A few minutes passed as he eyed the rest of the merchandise, then he met my eyes with a grin. "Very nice. I'll take them all. How much?"

"Market price for any of these is between three-fifty and four before tax," I told him, keeping my voice steady and without a single drop of emotion. "You can have them for two-fifty a piece." I sat and leaned back in my chair, crossing my arms over my chest. "Take it or leave it." Then I waited. I had no way of knowing if this would work or not, but I also had nothing to lose.

"Deal." Tony pulled out a large roll of hundreds, counting them before he handed them to me. Without thinking, I passed the money to Julio who immediately started counting it again. Tony eyed me. "I need more. Will that be a problem?"

"All here," Julio told me.

"As long as the money is real, I might be able to help you out," I replied.

"Lady, if we could counterfeit money, do you think we would be here?" Tony asked as he closed the briefcases.

"Good point." I had to admit he was right.

"Are you ready to be a rich woman?" Tony said, and I knew it was a prod to see if I would keep dealing with him since I'd never definitively answered him earlier.

"I have a couple rules," I said, sitting straight as I crossed my legs, making myself look as regal as I possibly could. "One: I don't do business with anyone but you. Two: You never come here unannounced. And three: All communication goes through Hector." I steepled my hands and planted my fingers under my chin.

"Simple enough," Tony said. "Anything else?" He looked deep into my eyes, waiting for my response.

"I'll need a three-day notice for orders to be fulfilled. No more of this last minute stuff. Agreed?" I made my voice hard, ensuring Tony could take my words as nothing other than an order.

"As you wish, Cat Lady." Tony smirked at his use of my nickname. "I'll text Hector the next order this evening, then. We'll need it first thing Friday." He grabbed his cases and held them at his sides as he met my gaze again. "Can we count on the Cat Lady Special again?"

"Of course, dear, what kind of business woman do you take me for?" I said with a soft smile.

"The kind that trains deadly felines and disguises them as innocent house cats," Tony said, peering around the patio. "Where are your killers, anyways?" he whispered, as if he was afraid my cats might overhear him.

"Watching you from the living room window, waiting to see if the twins failed so they can jump in and devour you." I pointed at the window behind me, not even having to look. I knew my kids were there, ready to attack.

"You are definitely one crazy lady, but I like you," Tony said with a smile. He put one of his briefcases down and extended his hand. "A pleasure doing business with you, Ms. Angela. This is the beginning of a great partnership."

I shook his hand. He had a firm grip, but his skin was rough and calloused. There was nothing soft or gentle about this boy.

"See you Friday, Tony," I told him as he grabbed his goods and headed towards the door. "Hector, please escort him out."

"Of course, Ms. Angela," Hector said in the most polite voice I'd ever heard come out of him. That was new...

I watched Hector and Tony walk away. As soon as they were out of sight, I slouched in my chair and dropped my head back. "Wow. That went well," I said to no one in particular, then I let out a heavy sigh that did wonders for my jittery nerves.

"You just made a deal with the devil and walked away with cash," Julio said, walking around me. He took the seat next to me and dropped the cash on the table.

I reached for the money but didn't touch it. I couldn't. It was more money than I'd ever seen in one place in my whole life. It meant I wasn't going to be homeless. It meant I could take care of myself, but it also meant so much more. Before I realized it, tears streamed down my cheeks, but I didn't even try to wipe them away. They were happy tears, and I didn't care who saw them.

"Ms. Angela, are you okay?" Julio asked, straightening in his chair.

"I'm fine," I said as I pulled out six bills from the pile. "Here. Three hundred for you and three for Hector."

"We can't take that," Julio said, waving his hands in front of him like he was on fire.

Just then Hector returned, staying at the door as he took us in.

I turned to him instead, knowing he wouldn't hold back. "Why not?"

"Our mother would kill us," Hector said, eyeing the money like a starving man coveted food.

"Mami won't take charity, even after she was hurt," Julio said, staring at his hands. "After she broke her back, we all take on odd jobs to help out. As long as it's work, she's okay with it. This is different, and that's why she is so mad with us."

I admired Ana, but I also knew she was a single mom with three kids. She lost her cleaning business after she got hurt and the only income she had now was selling food.

"Well it sounds like you two have work to do now," I told the boys as I piled the rest of the money up. "The Julio and Hector Handymen Company is now open to business. My lawn needs cutting, and my flowerbeds need up keeping, so get to work."

"Ms. Angela, that is not worth six hundred dollars," Hector said from the other side of the patio screen.

"What makes you think that's the only thing you will be doing?" I replied, crossing my arms.

"Go home and check with Ms. Ana and see if she is okay," I told the boys. "I have to go to the bank and save the house. I'll leave you a list with stuff to do, and it will be here when you get back."

"Ms. Angela, you don't have to do this," Julio said, wiping his eyes.

I grabbed his cheeks and made him look me straight in my eyes. "I have no idea what I'm doing, but I do know that when I was starving, your mom gave me food, even when she didn't have enough for herself." I paused and angled my head. "If this is going to work, then we are all going to benefit from it. You brought me the client, so you get a cut. Are you two okay with that?"

Julio only nodded, but Hector raised his chin. "Yes, ma'am. We won't let you down."

"I know you won't," I told them. "Hurry home, then. We got things to do." I got up and headed towards the house but stopped at the door as Hector ran ahead. Julio took the money, following his brother a lot slower.

It made me wonder if that money was the difference between eating and having a roof over their heads like it was for me. I'd ponder that later. Right now, I had bills to pay, and finally enough money to pay them with.

Chapter Six

There was a blessing that came with living in a small town: everyone knew everyone, each relationship meticulously built with the passing of time. It could also be considered a curse because it was almost impossible to keep anyone's business private.

Which meant going to the bank had turned into an hour and a half long excursion discussing my new endeavors and how exactly I had come into this new money.

Normally, I had the hardest time coming up with stories on the spot, and today was no different. When Jeff, my poor account manager at the bank, asked me about my current situation, I stretched the truth. He now thought I had opened an eBay store and sold goods on the internet. Close enough to the truth, and Daddy had always said, "The key to telling a convincing story is to scatter enough truth to confuse people." Which I had. Only the goods I was selling were not harmless items, and the sales weren't taking place online. However, the lie had made even more work for me. I now had to buy a computer and set up an eBay account.

I should be ashamed of myself for lying to poor Jeff, but drastic times called for drastic measures. Thanks to my family's reputation and years of patronage, my new loan was in the process of being refinanced to a more affordable one. It surprised me Jeff was VP at the bank. I was more than behind on my town news. It worked out, though, because he had the power to help me now. Of course, walking in with a stack of cash probably made him more than willing.

Funny how one week could change so much. This time last week, I couldn't even borrow a thought, nevertheless a loan.

Stop number two brought me to another place I had fallen behind on payments for. After months of debating, I'd decided the time had come to clear my storage facility at the far end of town. I had been holding out hope for Todd to come back and had placed everything he hated that belonged to my family away just to make him happy. I kept telling myself I kept it there for a yard sale, but who was I fooling? I hated yard sales, so I knew I'd never have one.

Two hours of sorting through memories later, I was exhausted, but I'd managed to find all the lost treasures from my youth, my favorite family heirlooms, and a few other sentimental objects that were on their way home with me. The rest of the stuff was heading to Joe's Pawn Shop. That would be a great job for my new handymen. Now that the account was settled, we could close the storage.

Joe's Pawn Shop's slogan was, "You got, I buy." It was also my last stop of the day. It always stumped me why Joe had named the place that, but I guessed it was different. His mom had made it into an antique store for a few decades, and the place had been filled with old, creepy dolls and more dollies that a museum could handle. When Joe had taken over, the dolls disappeared and the gun racks appeared. To this day, the pawn shop was the most profitable business in town. Not sure what that really said since we didn't have that many businesses to begin with, but his at least was the best.

"Afternoon," Joe shouted from the back.

"Hi Joe," I said as I closed the door behind me.

"Angela? Is that you?" Joe asked, but I had no idea from where. I still couldn't see him.

Peering around the shop, I made my way to the back of the building where his register was located. The pawn shop looked more like a metal barn than a store thanks to the renovations Joe had done. He had torn down the old house and enlarged it in the shape of a square, making it resemble a Walmart. How he kept up with his inventory was beyond me.

When I finally made it to the register, I found Joe next to some shelves in one of the aisles. He was a little older than me, around six feet two, but he had to be well over three-hundred pounds, which consisted of nothing but solid muscle. His thick black hair that had brought out his bright green eyes so well had started thinning a few years back. When that had happened, he shaved it, which made him look more like an angry bouncer on a pirate ship.

"There you are," I told Joe. "What are you doing?" I had thought he'd been stocking the shelves, but considering he was carrying a rag, painter's tape, and a ruler, I wasn't so sure now. Plus,

I had no clue how he could balance all that stuff without dropping any of it.

"I got new inventory coming in, so I'm marking the new location," Joe told me, pointing at the shelves. "I like things to be neat and in order, so getting the spot ready now."

I glanced at the strange shape and decided I didn't want to know what new merchandise he was making room for.

"Have you ever considered hiring more people?" I asked Joe, my gaze spanning the huge place.

"Are you submitting an application?" Joe asked, his eyes moving from my head to my feet almost in slow motion.

"Not right now," I told him. "I'm pretty sure I don't have enough upper body strength to work here." I pointed at the giant set of tires that were stacked next to one side of the register. "I don't want to know."

"No, you don't," Joe said.

"Great, now I want to know," I said, and I had a feeling he'd set me up for that. Every time anyone ever told me I didn't want to know something; it always got my curiosity going. I thought it was probably like that for almost everyone.

"Some crazy kid sold his parents' tires because they took his truck keys." Joe shook his head and frowned.

"Is that legal?" I eyed the tires like they were strapped to explosives and ready to blow.

Joe shrugged. "I don't ask a lot of questions here, and it was a fair deal. Unfortunately, I can't give the tires back to the parents until I get my money back, and according to the parents, their sweet little angel went to Shreveport with his friends and lost all the money at the boats." His grin had completely disappeared. "Which means these tires will have a new home as soon as I can find a buyer."

"I don't blame you," I told Joe. "What people are capable of sometimes blows my mind."

"You don't know the half of it." He shook his head again and chuckled, meeting my gaze. "But that's a story for another time. What brings you in today? Are you here for your rings?"

A sigh left me. Last month, I'd pawned my wedding rings to cover the utility bills, but even before that, I'd become a regular customer with Joe.

"Not at all. Keep those hideous things and make a killing." I stared him right in the eyes, showing him just how serious I was. It was past time I started being strong again.

"Angie, I'm so sorry." Joe's voice turned soft, gentle even. It always took me by surprise when he did that because he was such a big guy. "I read it in the paper."

"That makes two of us," I told him, and I had to will the shake out of my voice "What can I say? People move on. It's about time I do too."

"Good for you." Joe squeezed my shoulder. "Then what brings you here today?" His eyes twitched, and I figured the curiosity was killing him.

"I've been cleaning my storage unit and have tons of stuff I need to get rid of." I made my way to the counter and leaned on it, trying to think of a way to tell him the real reason I'd come.

"That's great. Do you have the stuff in your car?" Joe asked, peering over my shoulder like he could see all the way outside. Last I checked, he didn't have X-ray vision and he wasn't some kind of superhero, even though he might look the part.

"Not today," I told Joe. "I will be sending my new helpers Julio and Hector to handle it."

"Who?" Joe asked, crossing his arms like an over-protective mama bear.

"You know, the twins from my neighbor down the street," I told him, trying not to roll my eyes.

"Ana's kids?" Joe relaxed his shoulders again. "That is one hard working woman. She didn't deserve how that bastard treated her. The boys are helping you now?"

"I'm hiring them, yes," I told Joe.

"You are a good woman." Joe gave me a wink. "Tell them to swing by and I will take care of them."

"Thank you, Joe." My eyes were on the counter and I played with my purse, my nerves getting the better of me.

"Angie, what else is going on?" Joe moved to the counter, leaning on it and mimicking my pose.

"You used to do lots of business with my dad," I whispered.

"Your dad was a great man." Joe looked up, which was his way of honoring the man.

"I want to restart that partnership," I blurted out.

"What?" Joe popped up from the counter. "What do you know about my business with your dad?" He took a few steps closer to me and leaned down. I wasn't sure if he had done it to make sure our conversation didn't travel through the store, or because he might be about to clobber me.

I didn't back down, even though I had to hold my own hands to stop them from shaking. "I found all his notes."

"Guns are no kind of business for a woman." Joe's eyes darted around the store, and when they landed on me again, they were soft. "No offense Angie, but women don't know how to keep their mouths shut."

My mouth dropped open, kind of ironically proving his point. "I could say the same for men," I replied, somehow finding the courage to stand up straight. "I guess if that is the case, though, there's no reason for me not to tell Maggie about your little moonlight trips with her cousin. You know, since women can't keep their mouths shut anyway." I twirled my hair to add even more effect.

"How do you—" Joe started, but he stopped as he choked on his own spit.

"Joe, breathe," I slapped him on the back. "Don't die on me now."

"Angela, this could ruin me," Joe mumbled as his face turned an ugly shade of green.

"Joe, relax." I crossed my arms over my chest. "I have known for years, and that isn't the only dark and dirty secret I know. I've never said a word, though. Not once." I paused and touched his shoulder. "I'm not here to blackmail you, but I will if you give me no other option. All I want is to rekindle our business alliance. Easy as that."

"I'm not sure if I should be impressed or afraid." Joe gripped the counter. "What do you have in mind?"

"The same as my dad. A steady supply of guns that are clean and untraceable." I gave him my best million-dollar smile.

"You do know that until this day I had no idea what your dad did with all those guns." Joe glanced at his gun rack.

"We like guns. That's all," I said.

"Fine, I won't ask, and you won't tell." Joe extended out his hand.

"Very military." I shook his hand, closing the deal. "Just call me when you have something good."

"I know the drill, Angie," Joe told me. "Whatever you are up to, be careful. I know you are hurt but don't throw your life away to pay Todd back. He's not worth it."

I hated the fact that everyone assumed everything I did had something to do with Todd. Part of me also wondered if they might be right, but I didn't give voice to that part of my brain.

"Not this time Joe," I said. "It's time for me to move on and have my own life now." And this time, I planned to make sure it counted.

"Anything I can do for you today?" Joe asked, but he froze when the bell jingled at the front door. Then he shouted, "Afternoon."

"Hi Joe," a male voice replied.

After a few minutes, the other thing I needed came back to me. "I need a computer," I told him.

Both of Joe's eyebrows lifted.

"I'm opening an eBay business and need it," I told him, hoping he didn't ask any questions. I shouldn't worry. He was pretty good at not asking. Just about as good as I was at not telling.

"Do you even know how eBay works?" Joe asked me in a low voice.

I shrugged. "Not a clue." We looked at each other for a few minutes before we both busted up laughing.

"Oh Angie, you are full of surprises. Let me see what I have," Joe said and headed towards one of his shelves.

The day had gotten more interesting by the minute. Who knew I had the nerve to stand my ground? I'd never been one to go against the grain, and most people knew they could count on me to do the right thing. It made me predictable and boring. Now, a surge of excitement shot through my veins, and a light-headedness settled over me. I needed to head home and get a nap before all this excitement caused me to have a heart attack.

Chapter Seven

"Angela! Angela!" a voice shouted.

It had been a voice, right? I couldn't be sure, not when everything was fuzzy and I was so warm and comfy. It made me really not want to open my eyes.

"Angela, wake up!" This time I knew it was a voice, and that voice was screaming so loud it had made the ground tremble around me. It was way too early to deal with an earthquake.

I shouted and jumped into a sitting position, only to find Mother next to me, shaking me to death.

"Wake up," she repeated, and the veins in her neck pulsed.

"I'm up. If I'm not, then I'm having a heart attack, so there's that," I told Mother as I pulled my fleece blanket up from the floor.

"Why are you sleeping in the living room?" She glared at me.

I had finally woken up to return to the land of the living, but it might have been too late because Mother wasn't alone. Hector and Julio stood right behind her.

"Trust me when I tell you it will be the last time I ever do," I said in my most sarcastic tone. "Now, how did you get in?" Straight to the point. I was too tired to deal with Mother this early in the morning.

"I have a key," Mother jangled a set of keys in front of me, waving them around like a maniac.

"Yes, I know you have keys. That doesn't explain why you didn't you call first, though." A quick peek under the blanket told me I had at least put pajamas on. Good thing. I needed coffee.

"You weren't answering your phone," Mother said. "And after how strange you were acting yesterday, I got worried." She stood straight, crossed her arms over her chest, and cocked one hip to the side. I might be in my forties, but that pose still scared me to death.

"What are you talking about?" Yesterday had been a strange day from the start, so Mother needed to be a bit more specific. That way I could avoid asking the wrong question. My mind wasn't as sharp as normal, either, considering I'd spent most of the night awake doing inventory, leaving me completely exhausted now.

"Well, for starters, I'm talking about your visit to the bank in which you somehow are no longer on the verge of losing the house." Anger radiated from her, and I could've sworn she had started foaming at the mouth. "How could it be that I hadn't even known you were on the verge of losing the house, but now I'm left with even more questions. Like where you found the money to pay off your debts." She gestured to Julio and Hector. "Not to mention, you have these two mowing, trimming, and fixing anything and everything in disarray around the house." She tapped her foot against the floor. When that happened, it was always worse for me. I needed to calm her down and fast.

"Mother, you have too much stuff to worry about already," I said in a dismissive tone, then I stood and moved around her, making my way towards the kitchen.

"Where are you going?" she shouted at me.

"Coffee, Mother," I told her. "The stuff that makes every day just a little bit better."

"What day? It's almost noon," Mother said. I glanced at the digital clock on the microwave and sure enough, she was right. It read eleven-thirty.

I poured a large mug, but skipped the Irish Cream, hoping to eliminate anymore lectures from Mother. With coffee in hand, I struggled back into the living room and leaned against the door frame to wait for the verbal lashing I knew was coming.

"Are you going to explain?" Mother asked in that cold, hard tone people tended to get right before they exploded. "While you are at it, why do you need a computer?"

"I'm impressed," I told Mother as the sleep fog around my brain dissipated. "The rumor mill in Sunshine is out in full force and working overtime." I gave a salute with my mug.

"Angela, stop stalling. Speak up." Mother stared at me like a bull at a Spanish bullfight.

"I pawned a few things and got things back in order," I told Mother. "Nothing crazy."

"Don't feed me that bull, Angela," Mother hissed. "Nobody

gets fifteen hundred dollars at a pawn shop." She radiated evil. "Hector, spill it."

"Ms. Angela is selling guns," Hector shot out, even faster than a rapper.

"Hector!" I yelled back.

"Sorry Ms. Angela, but your mom is scary." Hector's eyes were on his feet. I didn't blame him. My mother *was* scary.

"Great job, Mother," I told her. "Your mere presence is now a force of terror to the youth. Hector's probably going to need therapy to treat his PTSD." Bringing my mug to my lips, I sipped my coffee and kept my eyes off my mother.

"Don't try to turn this around on me." Mother's voice turned a bit calmer. "Where did the guns come from and who did you sell them to?" Interrogation mode had returned.

"The guns were dads and the buyer is from a Mexican guerrilla," I said as I made my way to the sofa again.

"Your dad's?" Mother asked in a high-pitched voice. "Angela, your dad left you that stupid Smith and Wesson you adore. You couldn't have made that much money off that thing."

"Mother, there's something you need to see." I paused and turned around instead of sitting on the couch. "Hector, Julio, you are coming too. Check the perimeter and make sure nobody is lurking around the house, then meet us in the back yard. I'm going to get dressed first."

"Where are we going?" Mother asked, watching the boys dart out of the house.

"To Dad's cave," I told her as I headed towards my room.

This had definitely not been how I'd planned to spend my morning, but too late now.

Fifteen minutes later, the four of us were standing in front of the shed. Julio and Hector looked like they were being dragged to their execution, while Mother eyed the shed with disgust. To make matters worse, she kept rubbing her hands on her trousers like a dirt storm was attacking her.

"Angela, this is not funny," Mother said.

"Just trust me, Mother," I said as I unlocked the door. "Hector, Julio. Pay attention. This is part of your job. Never, ever let anyone near this shed. Got it?" I met their eyes right as they nodded, looking between the shed and me.

I opened the door and ushered the three of them inside. Once we were all in, I flipped the lock and made my way to the trapped door, pulling it open and turning the light that illuminated the stairs on.

Mother leaned in. "What is that?" She peered down the stairs, but I knew she couldn't see much.

"Remember Dad's bunker?" I asked.

She nodded. "But he told me he got rid of that thing and filled in the hole." Her eyes were buried in mine.

I took a deep breath. Hopefully she wouldn't choke me for the sins of my father. "He did *something* with it," I told her. "Let's go."

"What?" Julio's voice shook.

"We are not going in there," Hector shouted, but his voice cracked. "I've seen those movies. Every brown person always dies in them. No way."

"Well, my cowardly lion, I'm glad you have so much faith in me," I told Hector, who was backing up as far as the shed allowed him. "Stop being dramatic. Follow me if you want, but if not, just stay here." Without turning back, I stepped down the stairs.

Mother couldn't take the curiosity and followed. I wasn't sure what motivated the boys, but they were right behind her. When I reached the ground level, I turned on the light.

"Mary Mother of God," Julio whispered behind me.

"Holy Rambo! Your dad was the shit," Hector exclaimed.

"He put paneling here!" Mother yelled.

I turned toward her, crinkling my forehead. "What? Are you serious? That's all you have to say?"

I was definitely learning a lot about Mother's priorities.

"I couldn't get your dad to change a light in the house, and he has floating lamps here," Mother said. She eyed the room with rage. "I'm going to kill him again as soon as I find him in heaven. Look at that, he even added fake windows."

For the first time in my life, I was glad Dad was dead. Otherwise Mom would've put him in his grave right then.

"Mother, breathe. Please," I said, wanting to touch her but

afraid to.

"Oh, he is so dead. I'm going to kill him." Mother paced a circle around the room, her fists clenching and unclenching at her sides.

"Mother, Dad is already dead," I said, hoping my words would calm her down.

"Angela, don't mess with me." Mother gave me a pointed stare before she marched around the bunker. I was just happy to see her no longer stomping a circle into the floor.

"Ms. Angela, Mrs. Barbara looks ready to explode," Julio told me.

That was the understatement of the year.

After her fourth lap around the room, Mother's eyes fell on me. "I want in."

"What?" I raised my eyebrows, not sure if I'd heard her right. "What are you talking about?"

"Whatever you're doing, I want to join you," Her hands went on her hips.

"Are you serious?" I said, my tone much higher than it should have been.

"Do I look like I'm joking?" Mother asked.

"I have a feeling your mom never jokes, Ms. Angela," Hector said from behind me.

I hushed him, then turned to Mother. "Mother this is not a joke. We are dealing with dangerous people," I explained.

"How much did you make? And for what model?" Mother picked up a shotgun from one of the racks, checking the chambers like an expert weapons handler.

"Twenty-five hundred for ten 9mm," I whispered.

"Not bad. Maybe a little on the low end," Mother replied.

"It's the Cat Lady Special," Julio grinned.

"I like it." Mother took regal strides to another rack of AK-47s. "I'm miserable, Angela." Her words came so low, I almost missed them, but she had my attention. Julio's and Hector's, too, because they froze in their tracks and gave her a wide-eyed stare. "My savings are running out, my pension is so low it's barely there, the assisted living facility gets more expensive every year, and I have nothing to do there. I'm afraid if I stay, I'll lose my mind *and* develop dementia just from lack of excitement."

"Mother," I blurted. "You can always move back here. This

is *your* house." The words came faster than my brain could process them, but it didn't matter. Family always came first for me. When they needed something, I made sure they got it.

"Angela you were married," Mother said in an unsteady voice. "I'm not asking for charity, but I know as much about guns as your dad. Whatever you are doing, you can't do this alone. A single woman is an easy target."

With one glance at Mother, I knew she spoke the truth. If anyone ever found this bunker, they'd kill me to get inside.

"You are moving in today," I told her. Three pairs of eyes burned into me, but I only met Mother's stare. "Stop acting surprised. You're right, and I'm woman enough to admit it."

"You have never agreed to anything this quickly," Mother said as she inched towards me like I'd turned into a wild hog and she was afraid of an impending attack.

"I'm tired, I'm beat down, and I don't want to be alone anymore," I admitted to everyone. Tears fell. I could do nothing to stop them. "I need you." My heart rate tripled.

"Angela, honey," Mother said.

"This is not charity, but a business proposition, considering half of everything in here is yours too," I told her. "Here is my offer. Move in and help me run this, fifty-fifty after we pay bills and assistance," I said the last pointing at the boys. "I have no friends, but you are a social butterfly. Nobody would ever question people coming and going if you were here." I hated to admit the last part, but it was time for me to face my demons and move on.

"Anything else?" Mother asked.

"Just stop treating me like a child," I told her.

Mother beamed and rushed at me. I wasn't sure if I should run or scream. Before I could decide, she wrapped me up and held me tight, giving me a perfect view of Julio and Hector glancing between us and the exit.

"I've been waiting my whole life for the day you would liberate yourself and take a chance on you," Mother said as she pulled away, but she didn't let go of me. "I wasn't expecting arms dealer, but beggars can't be picky."

"You have some strange parents, Ms. Angela," Hector told me.

"Tell me about it," I replied.

"You two know I'm standing right here," Mother said,

inciting a giggle from Julio. At least one of us was smart enough to keep our mouth shut.

"Sorry, Mrs. Barbara," Hector mumbled.

"Better," Mother said. "What's next?" she asked me.

"I guess we swing by the assisted living and get your stuff," I told Mother. "We got an order for this Friday, so we need to get back to cleaning and organizing guns."

"Sounds great, but let's do lunch. Or is it breakfast for you?" Mother asked with a smile. "I know you don't mind skipping meals but the rest of us like food, so let me cook something up." Hector and Julio need to asked permission to join us." She pointed at the boys.

"We are going?" Julio asked.

"Of course, we need help carrying boxes," Mother said. "You don't expect two women to do all the heavy lifting. Not to mention, if you're going to be around, people need to get used to seeing you." I hadn't thought about the last part. We didn't need the rumor mill starting up about us.

"Good point," I admitted. "Let's get ready then. You two head home, then meet us for lunch," I ordered the boys, gesturing toward the stairs with a flick of my head.

Julio and Hector rushed out of the bunker. Mother walked around and laced her arms through mine.

"You do know I'm planning to kill your dad again," Mother said with a small smile. I just shook my head, and we moved in silence for several seconds before she added, "You do have friends, Angela, you just pushed them away. It's time for you to start living again."

Mother and I strolled arm and arm, and my thoughts were buzzing with excitement. I never expected to have my mother as a business partner. What an interesting turn of events.

Chapter Eight

Terminating Mother's contract at the assisted living place, or retirement community as they preferred to be called, was harder than breaking someone out of jail. They had forms on top of forms of stuff normal people would've never even considered. It made me wonder how hard it had been to get in.

Two hours later, we started emptying Mother's apartment. I had always thought the place was interesting. With all the different activities they had going on, how could it not be? But in reality, it had been a scheme to keep the clients busy so they never noticed how much they had to pay.

Due to the short notice of Mother's departure, the manager refused to give her deposit back. It had turned into quite an argument, and I feared for that young girl. Only those under the age of twenty-five were foolish enough to believe they'd win a battle with their elders. She might've won the first round, but Mother would be striking a counterattack soon enough. I just hoped the place wasn't closed down after she finished with them.

I was grateful for Julio and Hector's assistance. They looked like professional movers with their synchronized steps and their ability to pack boxes faster than anyone I had ever seen. For some strange reason, Ms. Ana was determined to make sure her boys earned their portion of the money. This translated to me having permanent bodyguards everywhere I went. Although I wasn't sure what they were expecting to happen.

After thirty minutes of watching the dynamic duo work, Mother asked, "How are you two so good at this?" I pretended not to pay attention as I folded clothes into a suitcase, but I was just as curious as Mother.

"Our uncle is a handyman and our mother sent us to help him when we could. Moving is just one of things he does," Julio explained.

"Translation: we have plenty of practice doing odd jobs," Hector replied as he wrapped a weird lamp with a towel.

"I called our uncle and he is bringing his truck to help us move the big stuff," Julio told us as he pulled two more containers from under the bed.

"You thought of everything," I told Julio as I sat on the suitcase to close it.

"After one look at this place, we knew we wouldn't be fitting everything in your car," Julio answered.

"Julio is right, Mother. I thought you said you downsized?" I said as I gawked at her pulling stuff from a huge armoire.

"This *is* downsized." She gestured around the room. "Do you know how hard it was going from a twenty-five-thousand square-feet house to this one-bedroom studio?"

I let my gaze roam the whole room. Observing at what she had from the perspective she'd just given me made everything appear a lot different. "I take it back. You did great."

"Great use of your space, Mrs. Barbara. Impressive," Julio told Mother, giving her a smooth head nod.

"Stop brown nosing and get back to work. This stuff isn't going to pack itself," Hector told his brother as he threw a pillow from across the room.

Before I could correct the boys, the doors busted open. Watching Minnie, Ethel, and Florence rush into the room was like watching a runaway Mardi Gras float. There were colors, beads, and feathers flashing everywhere. Poor Julio jumped out of the way before the trio ran him over.

"Please tell us it isn't true," Florence begged, grabbing Mother's right arm. The woman flaunted another pin-up outfit, this one a tight but classic dress that showed off her well-defined legs. How did she do it?

"Angela, are you pregnant?" Minnie grabbed me by the shoulders. I had no idea she was so strong.

"Pregnant? What are you talking about?" I asked Minnie as I squirmed to get away from her, but she held tighter.

"Why else would your mother be moving back home with you?" Ethel jumped in. I had expected more from my feminist superhero, but she hadn't made any grand gestures. It was kind of disappointing.

"Minnie, let her go," Mother jumped in. Julio and Hector made themselves almost invisible by packing boxes on the far side of the room and not facing the old ladies. "Angela is not pregnant. We are just going into business together."

"Business? What kind of business?" Ethel asked, inching closer and closer to her.

"Are you opening a brothel?" Florence asked and I felt my face go hot. Julio and Hector hit the floor, but if they were trying to hide their laughter, they'd failed. Their jiggling shoulders kind of gave it away.

"Of course not!" Mother shouted.

"Oh, that's a shame. I've been practicing my dance moves," Florence explained, busting out some sort of crazy maneuver.

I had no idea what people did at assisted living, but I think I'd gotten Mother out just in the nick of time. This place made people crazy for sure.

"A brothel would have been fun. This town is getting so boring," Minnie said, giving us a scandalous look.

"Oh Lord, save my soul," I whispered.

"Don't be such a prude, Angie. You know nothing ever happens here," Florence told me as she fixed her fabulous dress.

"Stop avoiding the issue. What business are you four into?" Ethel asked, pointing at the boys who were poking their heads out from behind the bed. "Yes, you two are included in this. It is really suspicious to see you here." Her hands went to her hips and I knew we were in trouble.

"We are just here to pack, Ms. Ethel," Julio said, making a big deal of folding the bedspread.

"You might be cute Julio, but you aren't fooling anyone," Florence added.

Before we could reply, Ethel had locked the door and was leaning on it. Florence was getting closer to Mother, and Minnie had a steel hold on my left arm. Unless Julio and Hector decided to jump out of the window, they were stuck with the rest of us.

"Oh, relax ladies. Angela discovered her daddy's secret life and is following in his footsteps," Mother told her crew.

"Oh wow. Was he a gigolo?" Florence asked.

"Why does your mind always go there?" Mother asked her.

"Late nights, mystery trips, and secret phone calls…gigolo fits the pattern," Florence said as she tapped her foot in defiance.

"Dad was not a gigolo and before you ask, I'm not going into that profession," I told Florence, and I could've sworn her lower lip curled out.

Mother needed new friends.

"Fine, not a gigolo. So, what was your good-for-nothing husband up to?" Ethel asked. She never had a good thing to say about any man. It made me wonder if she'd ever liked any of them.

"It seems dear-dead-husband was an arms dealer," Mother told the ladies as she went back to packing.

"Yes!" Minnie screamed.

"I'm impressed. Go Harold," Ethel said. My mouth fell open as I looked at her. Ethel must like her men in the category of dangerous and criminal.

"I knew there was a wild side to him. No wonder you married him," Florence said.

"When do we start?" Minnie asked.

"We?" I asked quickly. "*We* sounds like too many people. There is no *we* here," I said as I gestured between the ladies and us.

"Angie dear, you need us," Florence told me as she sauntered over to a chair and sat down, regal as a queen ruling over her court.

"What are you talking about?" I took a deep breath. This situation had spiraled out of control.

"Who do you think was running the clubs during segregation?" Minnie asked me, but I had no clue what she was talking about.

"Just because your daddy failed to have the spirit of entrepreneurship doesn't mean you should. We are in," Ethel proclaimed.

My brain was running out of arguments and I felt a headache coming on, so I rubbed my temples. This day was getting worse by the minute.

"Ladies, this is not a game. This is serious business and people can get hurt," I explained.

"Dying in a nursing home is serious and depressing business," Minnie told me. "What is worse than that? If we go to prison, they will at least feed us. I would be a granny with street credit."

"That's what I'm talking about," Hector said. I tried to glare in his direction, but Florence was tossing clothes around the room, making it impossible.

"You let us in, or we will tell every soul in this town," Florence told me after stopping in front of the armoire.

I covered my mouth with my hand. "Are you blackmailing me?"

"Of course not, dear," Ethel said. "My sister is just demonstrating how effective we could be in growing your business." I had stepped to the fifth floor of hell and was paying for some strange sin I didn't know I'd committed.

"I'm not going to win this, am I?" I finally asked.

"Sorry dear, they are pretty convincing when they set their minds to something," Mother told me. She didn't even bother arguing with her friends.

"Fine, but nobody can know and right now we only have one client," I told the trio. "We are technically not recruiting for more."

"Well the Silver Hair Gang have joined the business," Hector said with a huge grin. A horrible image of me wiping that smile away with a bar of soap flitted through my mind, but I tried to bury it. It wasn't easy, though.

"In an act of goodwill, we are donating our stash to the business," Minnie announced.

"What stash?" I asked, glancing at the Silver Hair Gang.

"I got four Glocks, three Berettas and at least three Sturm Ruger," Minnie told me with the same tone of voice most people had when they read their shopping lists out loud.

"You have that here?" Julio almost shouted.

"Of course, silly boy." Minnie winked.

"This place is wild," Hector jumped in. "Old people are out of control."

"Who are you calling old, Hector?" Florence asked from across the room.

Hector bowed his head in a sheepish look. "Sorry ma'am, no one." He went straight back to packing.

"I have something similar, but with a few Smith and Wesson, of course," Ethel added.

"Well it's settled," Minnie announced. I gave her a wide-eyed stare. I had no clue what she thought was settled. Until she added, "We need to give Barbara her goodbye gifts." With that final announcement, Ethel unlocked the door and disappeared out it.

"Julio, Hector, please help us carry these gifts for Barbara." Ethel said in as loud of a voice as possible. "You wouldn't want any old ladies hurting themselves." She was half way down the hallway when I gave the boys the head signal to follow.

"We are *so* in trouble," Julio told me as he rushed out the door.

"We have passed trouble," I told him as Hector rushed after Minnie. "Mother, what have we started?"

"We have given them purpose again," Mother replied as she watched her friends march down the hallway with their heads held high, like they owned the place. When Mother closed the door, she faced me. "Angela, besides you, nobody ever comes to see us here. Minnie and Florence's kids have left them here to die."

"Mother," I said through clenched teeth. "They could get hurt." My heart rate sped up at the idea of something happening to any of these ladies. Somehow, they'd wormed their way into my heart, and I thought of them as family.

"Angela, they could break a hip climbing out of bed and wouldn't have the funds to fix it," Mother tapped my cheek, showing me more affection in that one movement than she had ever done in her life. "Now they have a reason to get out of bed, which is all someone our age can ask for." She paused and gave me a soft smile. "Let's go. We still have a ton of packing to do and they'll be back soon."

Lord forgive me, I prayed to myself.

This was getting out of control, but could I afford to turn back? No, I couldn't because I didn't have anything to turn back to. I wiped my faced, took a deep breath, and faced the room.

The Silver Hair Gang had joined the business. That was all there was to it.

"Time to make some money," I whispered with a smirk.

"That's my girl," Mother replied.

At the rate we were moving, it was going to take us all day to move everything back to my house, so we picked up the pace. The boys' uncle showed up and he had extra help in tow. With their aid, the furniture, clothes, and very well-hidden guns were transported.

All in all, it took us a few hours to get her things moved. I put everything she needed in her new room. The rest went to storage.

I seized the opportunity to take advantage of the extra help. Uncle helped us move all my stuff out of storage and sent it to the pawn shop. The crew refused to take any kind of money for all their help, so I made Hector buy them dinner with the money from all the stuff I sold. It was the least I could do.

The day was a productive one, and I felt rather accomplished until I entered the living room and saw all the objects scattered through it. It could wait until tomorrow. I was too tired, and so was everyone else, so we called it a day.

Chapter Nine

My body ached all over. The cats woke me up before sunrise and I decided to stay up—more like didn't have a choice since I couldn't get back to sleep. It was going to take me some time to get used to sleeping in my old room again. With Mother in the house, I couldn't keep sleeping on the couch.

The smell of coffee woke Mother up, so we jumped right to work. By the time the boys showed up at the house at eight, we had organized most of Mother's stuff in the house. At first, Bonnie and Clyde were not happy with the new roommate, but then she bribed them with roast beef. In the blink of an eye, Mother went from public enemy number one to the cats, to their favorite play thing. Cats were fickle and definitely not very loyal.

I put Hector and Julio to work as soon as they arrived. The new order for Tony included over one-hundred pieces. Not a big deal for us with my bunker inventory, but the guns had to be pulled, cleaned, and packed. Even with all four of us working, it took the rest of the morning. Mother was a natural handling a gun, but Hector and Julio were a different story. Using a gun was different than conducting maintenance in one, and cleaning one might be even harder to master. The boys had to learn the basics of every gun in order to be helpful with the process. They were both fast learners so teaching them was a pleasure.

My back was hurting from moving all the guns. Leaning over them while cleaning probably hadn't helped. Too bad we still had a lot of work to do. The new inventory we acquired from the Silver Hair Gang required inspection, cleaning, and testing. I knew the quality of the guns Dad carried, and they were in pristine conditions. Some of the ones we picked up from the ladies looked more like antique collectibles than actual weapons. We needed to test them before adding them to the inventory. One or two guns wouldn't be a hard task, but since there were over seventy-five, I had a feeling it would take a while.

Mother decided we needed to test the merchandise before we wasted the time cleaning the pieces, so she arranged a drive to Bob's place. He'd been a friend of the family for as long as I could remember and had also been one of Dad's closest pals. He also had his own range built right on his two-hundred-acre property. Even though he still lived in Cass County, he wasn't really within city limits. That meant he could do all kinds of crazy things on his property. It often made me wonder what kind of wild life my parents had once been a part of.

Mother made us roast beef sandwiches and banana pudding for lunch. She packed a container for Bob, and we were off. I had to admit, Mother thought of everything.

About fifteen minutes later, I pulled into his gravel driveway.

Mother turned to me. "Bob is expecting us."

"Do you think Bob would ever consider paving this road?" I knew it wasn't actually a road, but as long as it was, it resembled one.

"Bob is still as antisocial as ever." Mother looked out the window. "Paving his driveway would be like him inviting the world to visit." She shook her head with a grin. "He would never allow that to happen."

"Does he live alone?" Julio asked from the backseat. His voice sounded distant, and a quick glance told me why. His open-mouthed stare was too focused on the land Mother had pointed out that belonged to Bob to really pay attention to much else.

"Bob has two boys. Unfortunately, they married a pair of sisters who were straight floozies." Mother peered at Julio over her shoulder. "He cut them off and has not seen them in years."

"Damn! That's harsh," Hector said from beside his brother.

"Hector, watch that language," I told him in a soft voice.

"You know I'm right, Ms. Angela. That is nuts," Hector continued without a single apology.

"Bob is old school," Mother said. "He also blames those marriages for the death of his wife."

"Now that makes more sense," Julio added. "Still harsh, but a lot more understandable."

The youth of the world sure had a way of surprising me sometimes. Even in those moments when they were so wise, they could still be completely immature.

"What happens when he dies?" Hector asked. "Are his kids going to fight over the land?"

That was a really good question. From my experience, things ended up pretty messy when property and money were left behind after a death.

Mother folded her hands in her lap. "Bob found an attorney in Texarkana who specializes in estate planning. He's doing his best to make sure the boys and those horrible wives of theirs get nothing. Even when he dies, he will teach them a lesson."

"Bob sounds like a bitter old man," Hector said.

"Actually, he is really nice and sweet," I defended.

"Ms. Angela, he is probably only nice and sweet to you," Julio said.

Mother laughed. "The boys are right. Bob can be a bitter old fool, but he loves you, Angela." She gave me a side-eyed glance, but I refused to meet her eyes.

"What is that supposed to mean?" I bit my lip, worry gnawing at me. I didn't know if I really wanted to hear their answer or not.

A minute of awkward silence passed, then Hector finally cleared his throat. "Ms. Angela, you are nice to everyone. Everyone likes you, even when they find out you're a weird cat lady."

"I'm a what?" I wished I could glare at Hector, but the driveway kept winding this way and that, making me have to stare ahead and pay attention.

"Honey, you know he is right," Mother said in a gentle voice. "You are looking a bit homely."

I didn't have time to get offended. Not when we'd reached Bob's house. "I'm not homely, and we will continue this conversation later." After I parked, I turned to find Mother and Hector, only to find them giving each other high fives. Poor Julio just sunk lower and lower in their seat.

Bob was at my door before I turned the engine off. He still had a spring in his step and moved with the ease of a man who was comfortable in his skin. In his seventies, he had shiny white hair— the kind that made men looked distinguished instead of old. He wore coveralls and cowboy boots.

As soon as I jumped out of my car, Bob gave me a huge hug.

"Hi Bob," I said, taking in the scent of cigar wafting from

him. It reminded me of my dad and made my heart smile.

"Look at you, Angie. You are so grown." Bob's eyes moved from my head to my feet.

"That's because I'm getting close to fifty," I replied, shooting a bright smile his way.

"You are still a spring chicken." Bob turned to face Mother as she climbed out of the car. He let out a long whistle. "It must be a cold day in hell to have the one and only Barbara Carter in this part of the woods."

Mother waved her hands at Bob. "You crazy old fool. You know I've been here plenty of times before." She moved around the car and embraced him. "You look good, old friend."

I made my way to the trunk of the car as Bob and Mother caught up. When the boys climbed out, they waved at Bob, but he pretended not to see them.

"I don't have to tell you this, but I'm going to anyway. You look more than good." He leaned back and eyed her. "I thought you were joking when you called and asked to come to the house."

"Do I look like the kind of person to be making jokes?" Mother planted her hands on her hips and gave Bob a once-over glance.

"You do have a point," Bob conceded. "You said you needed the range?"

"Yes, we just acquired a few new guns and we need to test them," Mother said.

Mother's definition was a lot different than mine. Seventy-five guns did not constitute a *few*.

"If you load the guns in the four wheelers, I'll take you down to the range," Bob said, pointing to the two vehicles behind him.

"We got it, Ms. Angela," Julio said as he grabbed two cases of guns. Hector followed right behind him, not saying a word.

When the boys were out of hearing range, Bob turned to Mother. "What's the deal with the two kids? Why are they not in school?"

Panic fluttered through my chest. I had a horrible time trying to dodge questions and I made a terrible liar. Bob had a good question. Why weren't Julio in Hector in school? Just as I opened my mouth to try to spew some crappy lie, Mother stepped up.

"Oh Bob, it's a really sad story." Mother laid her palm flat against her chest. "But to make a long story short, those poor boys quit school to work so they could help their families. After seeing them, Angela had an amazing idea to open an alternative school for families like them, who just need a little extra help. Julio and Hector are our first students."

I eyed my mother. I guessed she was a lot better than me at coming up with stories on the fly.

"Sweetie, that is amazing," Bob said, giving me a soft, heartfelt look.

I held in my sigh. If I was heading to hell for going along with the lie, Mother was coming with me for telling it, so I went with it.

"It was the only way to give them a flexible schedule and still help them finish," I said, following Mother's lead.

"Today we are working on life skills," Mother added.

"That is so impressive," Bob said. "In that case, let's get you all to the range. You have lessons to finish." He walked to the car and picked up a couple of the cases.

I pulled Mother over as Bob went to the vehicles. "Alternative school?" I whisper-screamed.

"Angela, we needed a cover for having two high school kids with us all the time, and this is perfect," Mother hissed. "Besides, Ana did tell me the boys quit school to help their mother. She is devastated about the whole thing."

"Perfect," I replied back. "But now we need to set this up before people start asking questions. Sunshine is too small to make a lie like that work," I told Mother, holding on to her arm.

"Stop worrying, dear. Just call Ethel and explain the new development," Mother told me. Ethel used to be the superintendent of the local schools. If anyone could make something like that work, she could.

This was just crazy enough to work. Now I just needed to tell the boys.

In less than ten minutes, we had all the vehicles packed with the guns and Bob's supply of ammo. I was grateful that Bob was a hoarder when it came to bullets. Otherwise we might end up broke during the testing phase.

Mother and I drove the four wheelers. Bob rode with Mother and ate the lunch she packed him while the boys rode with me. It had been years since I'd driven one these. I had almost forgotten how much fun they were.

After I put some distance between my four-wheeler and Mother's, I spoke. "When did you guys drop out of school?" I waited for an answer, keeping my eyes facing forward. Neither of them spoke, so I added, "Come on now. Even Mother knows. What happened?"

"Mom works really hard for us, and our father is not coming back..." Julio trailed off.

"We were going to lose everything, so we started doing odd jobs to help her out," Hector said in a low tone.

"We were planning to go back to school but with mom getting hurt..." Julio stopped again, but he didn't need to finish the rest. The kids had stepped up to cover the costs.

"Well I have good news, you are now enrolled in school again," I told the boys.

"What?" Hector shouted.

"What school?" Julio asked.

"It appears Mother and I are starting an alternative school, and you two are our first students," I told the boys.

"Can you do that?" Julio asked in a hopeful tone.

"Believe or not, yes we can," I told Julio, glancing back at him. "As soon as we get home, I'll call Ethel. Since homeschooling is a thing and counts, an alternative program won't be a problem." I took a quick right turn to keep up with Mother and Bob.

"Does that mean we are going to have homework and stuff?" Hector asked.

"You will have school work, but I'm not sure about homework," I said over my shoulder.

"Are we going to be able to get our high school diploma?" Julio asked.

"With Ethel involved, you will be applying to college before spring is over," I answered.

"Woohoo," Julio shouted.

"Great," Hector whined.

The difference in their attitudes was amazing. I found myself laughing at the boys. Less than three days ago, I had been planning my demise, now I'd turned into an arms dealer running a school.

No doubt about it. I was going to hell. And I wouldn't be getting the role model of the year award, either.

We spent the rest of the afternoon with Bob, teaching the boys how to fire a gun. That whole side hold the kids did in the movies had to go. Instead, I showed the boys the proper holding technique, how to fire a gun, and I even showed them what to do in the case of a misfire. Dad had always been determined that every member of our household knew how to use any type of gun around, that way when the Apocalypse came, we'd be ready. Due to that, Mother knew what she was doing. In fact, she was still a sharpshooter with any weapon she picked up.

Little girls played with dolls, but I played with shotguns and rifles.

Having Bob around made the work a lot easier. He was an expert with guns and was able to repair some of the broken ones. I even learned a few new tricks to disarm an assailant. The afternoon was productive in so many different ways. And when we went to load the car, Bob looked a lot happier than when we'd first pulled in.

"Angela," Bob said, pulling me aside from the group during our last trip to load. "If you are picking up your dad's business again, be careful."

"Did everyone know about Dad's business? What makes you think I'm getting into it?" I'd really thought it had been a secret, but I guessed it had only been a secret to his own family.

"Why else would you be carrying cases of guns to test?" Bob asked.

That shut me up. I couldn't think of a single argument.

He just smiled and continued. "Only those in the business knew about it. How do you think a bunch of kids from East Texas got out of poverty?" I shrugged. I'd never really thought about it. He rubbed his chin. "We moved a lot of guns across the borders. Many borders. Once people find out the Carters are back in business, people will come out of the woodwork. Be careful, honey." Bob gave me a huge hug.

"You are not planning to talk me out of it?" I asked Bob. Why weren't people trying to talk me out of this insanity?

"Things are rough for everyone. You do whatever it takes to get back on your feet," Bob told me. I guessed the rumor mill had reached all the way out here. "If you need anything, I'm here."

"I need my dad," I told Bob.

"If your dad was alive, Todd would be dead now," Bob said as a matter of fact. "It can still be arranged, you know." He looked around the place, gesturing to the amount of empty land he had.

"Thanks Bob, but I'll be okay," I told him.

"In that case, watch your back and make as much as you can as quickly as possible. Then get out," Bob said. "Got it?"

"Got it," I whispered.

"Angela, we're ready," Mother called from behind me.

"See you soon, Bob." I patted the side of his shoulder and then stepped away. Deep down, I had a feeling I'd be seeing quite a bit of him now, though.

I drove home fast. The whole time, Mother discussed a school schedule with the boys. My mind swam with information. I needed some quiet time with my cats. Some time to think.

Tomorrow was going to be an interesting day with Tony, which meant I needed to prepare my brain to deal with him. A long, hot bath was definitely in the cards this evening.

Chapter Ten

It was five am when I had finally rolled out of bed. Sleep eluded me all night, and when I did sleep, I had nightmares of silver-haired kids chasing me through the streets with rulers. Freud would have had a field day with my life right now. It was one thing to sell guns to save myself, but now I had Mother, the boys, and a gang of silver-haired ladies depending on me. There was only one question floating through my mind now: did I like it better then when I'd been alone and destitute? Absolutely! Plus, it was kind of nice to go to bed without worrying if someone would knock on my door and evict me.

If I wanted to keep the house, feed the cats, and help the boys and their family, worrying in bed was not the way. It was time to execute. I dragged myself out of bed and took a quick shower. Bonnie and Clyde followed me around after their breakfast. I had too much nervous energy to stay still. Mother had gone grocery shopping last night, so for the first time in months, I had a fully stocked kitchen.

Cooking had a way of calming my soul. Without thinking too much, I grabbed bowls and mixing spoons and let my mind wander. By the time Mother woke up around seven, the house smelled heavenly. I had made homemade biscuits with gravy. The bacon was in the oven staying warm. The homemade cinnamon rolls were frosted, the gooey frosting dripping onto the plate they sat on. I also had chocolate chip muffins and extra-large oatmeal cookies cooling on the counter.

Maybe I should've opened a bakery instead of an arms shop. Every horizontal surface in the kitchen was covered with cooling racks and some yummy concoction. I was stuffed when Mother strolled into the kitchen.

"Busy morning?" Mother asked as she inspected my dishes.

"Couldn't sleep," I replied, licking frosting from the side of a bowl.

"I guess I should be grateful you didn't decide to vacuum instead," Mother said. She still wore her midnight blue nightgown, and as she made her way to the stove, I couldn't believe how she managed to look regal in sleepwear.

"Bacon is in the oven," I told her.

"Of course it is." Mother eyed the cinnamon rolls. "With all this food, of course you have bacon."

"Thanks, Mother," I replied, watching as Bonnie and Clyde followed her. She opened the oven and gave both cats a large piece of bacon.

"By the way, I'm pretty sure bacon is not good for cats," I added.

Bonnie and Clyde growled at me.

"You better close your door tonight or your children will poke your eyes out," Mother said as she pointed to the cats. "Not to mention, according to my doctor, bacon is not good for anyone. So we might as well share." She grinned as she fed the cats even more bacon.

I went to the cupboard and grabbed a plate for Mother. While she was munching on bacon, I prepared a plate for her with biscuits and gravy, cinnamon rolls, and a muffin.

"This is the kind of stuff you used to make when you wanted something," Mother told me.

I smiled casually, remembering those days. "Not today, Mother. I just don't want to get us all killed," I admitted to her.

"Nobody is going to die, dear," Mother replied with the confidence that only a southern lady could muster when facing hell. "But if a gun fire breaks out, just know we have more weapons than the enemy." She took a bite of her roll.

"You are not worried at all?" I asked, my voice not at all confident.

"Angela, you have always been smart, beautiful, and talented," Mother said. She faced me and my face warmed, then she continued. "Your dad and I have no clue why you settled for that two-timing loser. You put his sorry ass through school and pushed him to be better than he imagined. I know you, Angela. Even if you don't know yourself. So stop doubting yourself. It's time for you to make money."

I only stared at her in response. She'd left me speechless. Mother had never been one to give pep talks, but I had to admit I was grateful for this one.

Mother strode out of the kitchen carrying her plate with Bonnie and Clyde right on her heels. They probably thought she'd feed them more. Heck, she probably would. Honestly, it was hard for me to guess what Mother would do next, almost as difficult as it was for me to believe she thought so highly of me. My whole life I'd thought I'd been nothing but a disappointment to my parents. When had that changed?

I'd been so deep in thought I hadn't seen the boys rush through the back door, but I jumped when my eyes landed on them.

"Are we having a bake sale, too?" Hector asked as he reached for a cinnamon roll, but Julio slapped his hand before he made it all the way. "Ouch."

"Don't be rude," Julio chastised his brother.

"No need for that. We have plenty," I told the boys. "Bacon is in the oven," I said, making my way towards cupboards.

"Ms. Angela, are you okay?" Julio asked, eyeing all the food items taking up most of the kitchen.

"I'm fine, why?" I asked him as I grabbed more plates from the cupboard.

"You have enough food to feed an army," Hector responded.

"I couldn't sleep so decided to bake," I replied, not watching either boy.

"That's funny." Hector chuckled. "When I can't sleep, I play video games. I've never gotten up to bake." He shoved food in his mouth as he spoke.

"You couldn't bake, even if you wanted to," Julio corrected his bother.

I handed each of the boys a plate and watched them fill it to the top. I pulled the bacon from the oven. Bonnie and Clyde must've smelled it because they were rubbing against my legs.

"Mother has you two spoiled," I told them, but I still gave them another piece. I couldn't be the evil mom in the house. Purrs met my ears as they chomped away.

"Ms. Angela, what do you need us to do before the pick up?" Julio asked in between bites.

"We need to wipe everything down one last time," I told the boys. "Make sure to wear gloves. I left a bunch of pairs next to the cases. We need to make sure no finger prints can be found on the merchandise."

Both Julio and Hector nodded in agreement, even while the latter licked his fingers to get the remnants of the frosting from his cinnamon roll in his mouth.

"Tony said he will be here no later than ten," Hector told us. "We should have plenty of time to triple check everything."

Julio agreed with his brother. Maybe I wasn't the only one with nervous energy today. These boys had never triple checked anything in their lives.

"Let's go, Hector," Julio told his bother.

"How about you two finish eating and then start cleaning," I told them. "We don't need sticky handprints all over everything." I gestured to the cinnamon rolls.

We made idle chatter while we finished breakfast, and then the next two hours we spent inspecting and wiping weapons down as we feasted on sweets. We finished with an hour left before Tony would make his appearance, and that time moved in slow motion. Maybe backwards. I knew the clock was ticking but it didn't feel like it was going anywhere.

Mother joined us at nine thirty, as regal as Queen Elizabeth. "Angela, breathe. You are stressing the boys out."

I glanced at Julio and Hector. Mother might be right. Julio was gnawing on his bottom lip and Hector kept playing with his hair. Which meant I must be making everyone nervous.

"Sorry guys," I told them in a low voice as I loosened the muscles in my shoulder. "I just hate waiting."

"Waiting is part of the game," Mother told me.

"Fine," I replied, then I took several deep breaths.

"Those are supposed to be good for you, so keep breathing," Mother told me. "What's next?" Her gaze moved past me and landed on the boys.

"We might as well move everything to the patio," I told the group. "Don't forget to wear gloves."

It didn't even take us five minutes to get everything moved to the patio.

With our tasks out of the way, I let myself focus on the beautiful day. A soft, cool breeze whooshed around me, making the few leaves on the trees trickle to the ground. It had a calming effect on me, so I kept watching. By the time Tony showed up, we were all pacified and relaxed. He walked into the patio room carrying a brief case, but he stopped and stood by the door.

"Should I be worried?" I asked from the chair I sat on.

"I think I should be the one asking if I should be worried," Tony almost whispered. "You have a new guest it seems."

"Yes, I apologize," I told Tony, but in truth I wasn't that sorry. "Tony, meet Mrs. Barbara, and Mother, meet Tony," I made the introductions, pointing at each specific person when I spoke.

"Your mother?" Tony asked, giving her a careful look.

"Is there a problem, young man?" Mother asked, staring directly into Tony's eyes.

"Nothing at all ma'am. I just wouldn't have guessed you were mother and daughter. Maybe sisters." Tony shrugged.

Mother glowed under the compliment. They boy was smooth, I'd give him that.

"Are we done flirting?" I asked Tony and Mother in passing. "I got things to do and would like to complete this transaction before dinner time." I gave them a closed lip smile, hoping they didn't ask any more questions.

"Of course, Ms. Angela. It's always about business," Tony told me in an almost mocking tone.

I gritted my teeth while I considered clocking Tony right in the mouth.

"Boys, please bring the cases for Mr. Tony to inspect," I told Julio and Hector.

"Fuck me! You did it," Tony exclaimed.

"Watch your mouth, young man," Mother chastised. I was glad she'd said it before me.

"My apologies, ma'am," Tony told Mother and she nodded in acknowledgement. Then he added, "I'm just impressed you got them all so quickly."

"We are good; what can we say?" Mother shot out.

The boys lifted each case onto the table. We were able to fit all the guns in only eight cases. Which reminded me, I needed to put an order in for more cases. They were flying off my shelves.

When Tony's eyes fell on Julio's and Hector's glove-covered hands, I said, "Call it preventive measures. No finger prints."

Tony examined each case carefully. The rest of us waited. There was no turning back now, so no reason to be nervous. Tony finished with his check of each case in under ten minutes. Not bad at all. He knew what to look for when it came to making sure the guns were legit. No serial numbers anywhere on the guns that could be traced.

"Ms. Angela, this is outstanding. What's my total?" Tony asked as he grabbed the briefcase he'd left by the same door he came in from.

We all tensed a bit. This was the real test. What would he do after he got all the weapons?

"I promised you a deal: one hundred pieces of handguns, shotguns, and a few semi-autos, and all for just thirty-five." I crossed my arms over my chest. This could end really badly, so I waited with bated breath.

Julio snuck behind me, and Hector moved behind Tony, blocking the door. If he was planning a shootout, Tony wouldn't be making it out alive.

"It is a pleasure doing business with you, Ms. Angela." Tony rubbed his hands together, then he placed the case on the table and opened it. By the look on Hector's face, I had a feeling the briefcase was loaded with cash. My suspicions were confirmed when he pulled stacks of money out of the case and placed them on the table.

I handed the cash to Julio and Mother to count. I needed my hands free in case I had to draw my gun. Patting my lower back, I made sure my Smith and Wesson was still tucked inside my new jeans. It was, which made me feel much more reassured.

Silence encompassed the room while the money was counted.

After a few tense moments, Mother finally announced, "All here."

"Mr. Tony, it was a pleasure," I told him and reached my hand out to shake his. For thirty-five thousand dollars, I would've given him a hug.

"We're going to need of a large shipment two weeks from today," Tony told us. "Would you be able to deliver at least three times this quantity?"

"Of course, we will," Mother answered before I had a chance.

"We will have to make some deals, but we can make that happen," I added. I didn't want Tony to know that I had that kind of fire power on the premise.

"In that case, do your magic. I'll be seeing you in two

weeks," Tony said, grabbing his suitcase and one of the gun cases. "Could I borrow your assistants to carry these outside?" He glanced at the boys.

"Of course," I answered. "Hector, just make sure our dear neighbors aren't looking this way." Last thing I needed was the rumor mill going crazy.

"Will do," Hector replied and grabbed two of the cases. Julio was right behind him with two of his own, then they headed out.

"I don't trust that boy," Mother whispered as she watched Tony walk away.

"Anything specific, or just everything about him?" I asked, wondering what was setting Mother off this time.

"It might be the fact that he dresses like a thug," Mother said as Hector ran back in for the last batch. He grabbed the last two and jogged out the patio door. Mother frowned as she watched him go.

"What's wrong?" I asked.

"Hector and Julio need a makeover," Mother said as the boys came back in.

"Hey, I heard that," Hector said to Mother.

"Good. That means I don't have to repeat myself," Mother replied. "This wanna-be-thug look is not appropriate for law abiding young men." She pointed at their clothes.

"What are we supposed to wear?" Julio crossed his arms and angled his chin toward her.

I didn't want to be involved in that conversation, so I made myself busy dividing funds. I didn't care one way or another what anyone wore. It wasn't easy to block the conversation, but I managed it and figured out how to divide the money. We needed to put some of the money back into the business. Cases needed to be purchased, as well as more cleaning supplies, ammo, and guns. I took five from the top for the business, five for each boy and ten for Mother and me. Since the guns were coming from our stock, it was only fair. When I sold the weapons from the Silver Hair Gang, they would get their cash too.

"Okay everyone," I said, interrupting the discussion.

"Did you hear us?" Mother asked me very sternly.

"Sorry no, I was counting," I told her, shrugging.

"At least you are honest," Mother said. "What did you figure out, then?"

"Here you go. Ten for you, five for Julio, five for Hector,

five for the business, and ten for me," I told all three of them. "Any questions?" They were stunned silent.

"Honey, that's too much for us," Mother finally said. "Those are all your guns. Your dad left them to you."

"Ms. Angela, your mother is right," Julio said with eyes so wide they looked like they might pop out of his head.

"What do you think, Hector?" If anyone would ever tell me the truth, it was Hector.

"I have never seen that much money all at once in my whole life," Hector answered still staring at the pile. "I don't deserve it." Tears rolled down his cheeks.

"Well we are a sad group of criminals," I told them in a teasing tone, inciting laughter from them all. "Mother, you are right. They are my guns and I can do whatever I want with them, and the money from the sale. It's my turn to bless you guys, that way you can all bless others. We are in this together now. Besides, as we keep growing, our cut might be smaller, so enjoy it now." I grabbed my cut and the business's cut.

"Mom is going to freak out," Julio told Hector, still not touching the cash.

"Then you better run straight home and give it to her," Mother told the boys and they both beamed at that idea.

"By the way, do I want to know what you were all discussing?" I asked them before heading inside the house.

"We agreed the only way the boys were getting a makeover was when you got one," Mother told me with a wicked grin.

"What?" I stopped and stared.

"We are heading to Texarkana tomorrow for a little shopping spree," Mother told me as she grabbed her cash. She came over and kissed my cheek. "Love you dear."

"We are so dead," I told the boys.

"We know," replied Julio.

"Hurry home," I told the boys. "Don't be walking around with all that cash." They grabbed the money and rushed out of the patio, but I could see their wide grins a mile away.

I had no idea what I was doing, but I knew it felt good to see those smiles. I wanted to bring more to the people around me, and if selling arms made that happen, then I would embrace it every day. Now I needed to meet Ethel at the school system and get this alternative school set up. Maybe if I blocked the idea of heading to

Texarkana tomorrow it wouldn't happen. No, not a chance. It would happen whether I wanted it to or not.

Chapter Eleven

*G*t had been years since the last time I'd visited the school administration building. Sunshine was such a small town that we barely had a grade school. The students in middle school, junior high, and high school were farmed out to different districts. I had no clue where Julio and Hector had been attending high school. Navigating the education system in this county required a PhD in insanity. Instead of going crazy trying to figure everything out, I let Ethel do the hard work.

Ethel had been the superintendent of the Atlanta Independent School District for years. She knew everyone in every district and knew rules I'd never even dreamed off. Ethel was also fearless, and people did things for her just to avoid getting their heads chopped off.

We met for lunch at twelve thirty at a small Mexican restaurant in Atlanta. Ethel was addicted to guacamole, so this was the easiest way to thank her for all her work.

"Angela, what exactly are you planning to do with this little project?" Ethel asked me after finishing off at least twenty chips filled with guacamole and the hottest salsa I'd ever eaten.

"I have no clue," I admitted to Ethel as I mixed my half-sweetened, half-unsweetened tea.

"How does that work?" Ethel asked as she shoveled chip after chip in her mouth. Not sure why she was acting like they were almost gone. The restaurant served unlimited chips and salsa as part of the menu, but I knew better than to point that out.

"This is Mother's idea," I told her.

"That part makes sense," Ethel mumbled in between bites. She swallowed her chips and followed it with a large gulp of sweet tea before continuing. "If anyone can come up with crazy schemes, your mother can. Why did Julio and Hector drop out again?"

"To help their family survive," I told Ethel in a gentle voice. Truthfully, I couldn't be more impressed that these young men would make such a noble sacrifice. It said a lot about them.

"I got a copy of their records and they had pretty good grades," Ethel told me.

"They gave you their records?" I asked Ethel as I stopped playing with my tea.

"Are you planning to eat or just play with your food?" Ethel asked, eyeing the large plate of enchiladas sitting in front of me.

"Don't be changing the subject now." Ethel was a pro at the art of evading.

"I don't know what you are talking about." Ethel spooned more guacamole on one sad, little chip. Since her chimichanga had disappeared, she'd gone straight back to the chip basket.

"Ethel, what did you do?"

She avoided my eyes like the plague. "I kind of told the ladies at the administration building that you were starting a small, private alternative school and I was one of your teachers," Ethel told me as she put the chip down.

"That is perfect," I said in an excited voice.

"You aren't mad?" She gave me a hooded look.

"As long as you are actually planning on teaching, then of course not," I told her as I almost bounced off my chair. "I don't like the idea of running an alternative school but having you on staff would make the process so much easier. Not to mention Julio and Hector would actually get a degree."

"You are serious about this?" I wasn't sure which one surprised me more, the question or the disbelieving tone Ethel gave me.

"Of course I'm serious," That statement came out louder than I intended, causing people from the surrounding tables to turn and stare. After I cleared my throat, I lowered my voice. "I know Mother was creating a cover story to keep the suspicion off us. It's a great idea. Plus, those boys have made so many sacrifices for their family, and now we can help them."

"Why do you want to help them so bad?" Ethel asked in a soft voice.

"I don't know," I admitted. "I guess I want them to be better than me. I would like to see them achieving their dreams instead of giving everything up for others."

"Do you think they are not happy?" Ethel asked as she started on her chip again. I had no idea where she was putting all that food.

"I'm sure they are happy helping their mother, but nobody wants to feel trapped," I answered. "Just think of all the things they could do if they were in a better place."

"Do you regret all the sacrifices you made for Todd?"

Ouch. I hadn't been expecting that question, so I took a bite of my enchilada and stalled for time. Luckily enough, Ethel didn't seem to be in any rush.

"At the time, no," I said, and that was the truth. "When I was making sacrifices for our family, I was okay with it all. I dreamed of the day when we would adopt a child, and I knew everything would be worth all the struggles when that day came." I'd just unleashed one of my deepest secrets. I couldn't have children, but it had always been my dream to adopt. Unfortunately, my ex had never had any of the same dreams I had.

"Are you sure that isn't the real reason you want to help the boys?"

I had no idea why, but Ethel seemed to be on a mission to psychoanalyze me.

"I'm a little too old to adopt kids now, so the answer is no, Dr. Phil," I told Ethel.

Ethel giggled in response. "Relax Angela." She took a bite of her food and met my eyes, giving me her undivided attention. "I became a teacher to help kids because I couldn't have any. Whatever your reasons, don't apologize. Just know you are doing a good deed." She squeezed my hand from across the table.

I never knew Ethel couldn't have kids, but in that moment, I no longer felt alone. That was a bit foreign to me, but it also kind of calmed me.

"We are doing this?" I asked, but I didn't need an answer. I already had one.

"Paper work has been filed and we are doing this," Ethel replied. "Just be prepared once the word spreads because more kids will come knocking at your door. Are you ready for it?"

"More?" I asked as I looked around the place, imagining kids hanging from the ceilings.

"More," Ethel replied.

"Let's cross that bridge when we get there," I told her.

"That sounds like a yes," Ethel said and waved at our young waitress to get the check.

"Is this going to be one ticket or two?" The perky waitress asked as the red, purple, and blue highlights bobbed in her hair.

"One, please," Ethel answered. "My boss is treating me to lunch." The young girl handed me the bill and bounced to her next table.

"You are good," I told Ethel as I searched my bag for my debit card.

"I have learned many lessons from your mother," Ethel said, and I just nodded at her.

"Ms. Ethel, is that you?" a female voice said over me.

"Hi Sallie, how are you?" Ethel said.

When I looked up, I met the smiling eyes of a girl in her mid-twenties with bright red hair and freckles speckled on her cheeks.

"I can't believe you remember me," Sallie said, beaming.

"I make it my business not to forget a face. Or a name, for that matter" Ethel replied. "How are you?"

"I'm doing great. I got a job working on the campaign for county judge nominee Todd Parker," Sallie said, the words coming faster than any southern girl I'd ever heard.

I stopped listening to Sallie as I processed the information she'd just dropped on me like a two-thousand pound weight. I had no idea if it was the fact that my ex was planning to run for office or how fast the words had rushed out of her that had me speechless. Oh, who was I kidding? It was definitely the ex part. I watched Sallie walk away and was proud I at least waved goodbye, even though I couldn't make myself stop shaking.

"Angela, are you okay?" Ethel asked as soon as we were alone.

"He is running for office now?" The words were choked out of me, squeezed from the throat of a woman who'd just swallowed something jagged and sharp that had probably punctured a lung or something

"Angela, breathe." It was more of an order from Ethel than a request. "You cannot fall apart now."

"I could barely pay my mortgage, yet he has money to run a campaign," I said on an exhale, trying not to break down. "How is that fair? His life is perfect."

"Angela, life is never as perfect as it seems," she started, then she moved closer and squeezed my forearm. "Don't you dare feel sorry for yourself. You are not helpless, and you *can* do something about this."

"What? Run for office?" I joked in a sarcastic tone.

"Close," Ethel said.

I stopped shaking. Ethel now had my undivided attention. "What are you talking about?" My eyes moved around the room as I tried to make sure nobody had noticed my almost-breakdown. Ladies did not breakdown in public in Texas.

"Barbara said you made a killing this morning." Ethel leaned even closer. "How about sponsoring the opposition and making sure Todd doesn't win?" Ethel had the wickedest smile glimmering from her face.

"Are you serious?" I was hoping she had lost her mind.

"Just think about it for a few days," Ethel whispered. "Our current county judge, the absolutely handsome James, is running for re-election. Wouldn't it be great if you joined his campaign team?"

"Ethel, I have never worked on a campaign," I said, but what I actually wanted to say was, "I have nothing to add to a political group."

"You never sold guns before and you made a killing today." She shot me a grin.

I hated when Ethel had a point.

"We are at war Angie, and we are not letting that bastard Todd win. He got the first round, but vengeance will be ours."

I never realized how much my divorce had affected everyone around me. Todd had made some lethal enemies when he'd hurt me.

"This is crazy," I finally told her.

"Yes, and so is selling weapons. Does it look like we are stopping anytime soon?" Ethel stood from her chair. "You think about that. For now, I've got to run. I'm supposed to take Florence to her hair appointment."

"Thank you, Ethel," I told her as she kissed my forehead.

I watched Ethel march out of the door with holy determination. It made me hope that one day I'd be able to find her level of focus and strength. As I patiently waited for my waitress, I pondered the idea of going against Todd. What did I really have to lose? He'd already taken everything.

A little payback sounded good right about now.

Chapter Twelve

Lately, most of my free time was spent in the bunker. A sense of solitude and peace filled me the moment I stepped inside. Every time. How crazy was it that I felt such calm in a room covered with guns?

As I made my way around the room, I marked potential guns for the next delivery. Dad had an incredible inventory and had catalogued most of the guns inside his bunker. I'd found binders broken down by handguns, rifles, semi-automatics, and projectiles. Unfortunately, the catalog stopped two years before his death. I knew Dad was still buying guns up to the week he died, but for some unknown reason, he'd stopped logging them.

Updating the catalog would be a great project for the boys. It might take them a while, but it would make our lives much easier. Trying to figure out where over five-hundred guns were had turned in to a nightmare, and that wasn't even counting all the ammo.

As I went through, I put sticky notes near all the weapons I was considering for the next deal, and by the time I finished, it was close to seven in the evening. That actually made sense, since my stomach was protesting about the lack of food I'd given it today.

I was expecting an empty house when I made my way back up to the surface, but that wasn't the case at all. Mother had returned, and she had brought company. Maria, Julio and Hector's sister were all having dinner with her—at least I assumed it was dinner since they all had empty plates in front of them.

"She's alive," Mother said as she smirked at me.

"Hi Mother, Maria," I said to both of them.

"Hi Ms. Angela," Maria replied.

Maria was a beautiful young lady in her early twenties. The oldest of the three kids, she was thin and about five four. She used to have dark, silky hair almost to her waist, but last summer she took a trip to New York City to visit some distant family and came back with shoulder length hair and highlights.

"You are doing well dear," I told Maria as I made my way towards the kitchen. Mother had made chicken spaghetti and the house smelled amazing. Plus, I might be a little addicted to it. I also loved when other people made it for me.

"Thank you, Ms. Angela," Maria said. "Mother sent me. The boys told her you were getting a makeover and I'm here to help."

I froze mid-way to the stove. "Excuse me." My voice came out high-pitched as I turned to face Maria's and Mother's smiling faces. "Okay what am I missing?"

"I spoke with Ethel," Mother explained. "She told me about Todd." When she paused, I bit the inside of my cheek and just stared at her. She angled her head and continued. "I agree with Ethel. Joining James's campaign team is a great idea. But you can't do that looking like an old hag. Nobody will take you seriously. We have teenagers that look more put together than you." She eyed me, starting at my head and moving down to my toes.

"Thanks a lot. Why don't you tell me how you really feel," I said in my most sarcastic tone.

"Angela, it's time to move on," Mother told me.

"How is a make-over going to help with that?" I asked, trying not to pout. This felt like an assault on my self-esteem. It made me wonder if this might be what an intervention made a person feel like.

"Ms. Angela, I can make you look twenty years younger," Maria answered, crossing the room to reach me. Before I had time to run away, she yanked the clip out of my hair. You are in serious need of a haircut. Highlights will spruce that hair right up, too. And, I think a face mask will do wonders." She played with my hair.

"Golden highlights would look great with her complexion." Mother hopped to her feet and stood next to Maria. She crossed her arms over her chest and examined my hair.

"Some red would look great on her, too" Maria said.

"None of my clothes would go with those colors," I protested.

"Speaking of clothes, yours are hideous," Mother told me.

"Were you in my closet?" I asked as I planted a hand over my chest and backed away, but I couldn't because I was trapped between Maria and Mother.

"I know it's a horrible invasion of your privacy, but I needed some hangers," Mother stated in a plain voice. "Then I couldn't help it. Your closet is like a car accident you can't look away from."

"That bad?" Maria asked, but her eyes weren't on Mother. They were still on my hair.

"Honey, it is so out of fashion that she would be a poster child for 'What Not to Wear' if the show was still on," Mother said as if I wasn't standing right next to her.

"Mother!" I shouted in disbelief. "It is not *that* bad." At one time, I'd really loved that show, but in this moment, I really didn't appreciate the reference to it.

"Do you own any trousers?" Mother asked as she tugged on the bottom of my skirt. "Dear, it isn't like you are Amish?"

"I own a pair of jeans, thank you very much," I told Mother, jerking away from her grasp.

"You do?" Maria asked, starting down at my legs. "Have you ever worn them?"

Okay. She had a point. I looked at the floor when I replied, "Once, three years ago."

"Doesn't count," Maria told me. "Ms. Angela, you are a very beautiful lady, but we need to bring it out. Right now, you are making Bonnie and Clyde look bad."

"Meow," a pair of cats replied. I wasn't sure where my cats were hiding at, but obviously they were not that far away.

"Traitors," I said to the cats.

"Meow, meow." I glanced down to find both cats moving circles around my legs. Where had they come from? They hadn't been there a minute ago.

"Are you two trying to tell me I need a makeover as well?" I asked the cats as I bent down in front of my kiddies.

"Meow," Bonnie replied and got on her hind legs to kiss my face.

"It's unanimous. It seems we are all in agreement," Mother exclaimed.

"I'm not winning this, am I?" I asked both Maria and Mother.

"Not a chance," Mother replied.

"Fine, let's do this before I change my mind," I told them.

"Yes!" Maria squealed.

I was pretty sure this was the worst decision I'd made today, but I had run out of options. It had been years since I'd gotten a real haircut. Most of the time, I was too busy trying to save money, so I trimmed my own hair. Maria dragged me to a chair at the small dining table.

"By the way, you have no choice in this, so I don't want to hear any arguments. We are going to Texarkana tomorrow," Mother told me.

"Why?" I asked, unable to move around to face her since she'd pinned a hair-bib around my neck and had started to cut.

"You have no clothes," Mother told me.

"What?" I tried to turn, but Maria hit me over the head with her comb. "Ouch."

"Do you want to end up with no hair?" Maria asked me.

"No," I whinnied. I was feeling like a kid at the principal's office.

"In that case, stop moving," Maria scolded.

"Mother, what happened to my clothes?" I asked her, trying to remain calm and not move a single inch.

"We donated some and threw the rest away," Mother said as she took a seat in front of me.

"What?" I yelled.

"Stop moving!" Maria screamed.

"Relax," Mother said, waving at me like it was nothing. "We will get you a whole new wardrobe that actually matches a woman your age. No more hideous articles of clothing allowed."

Hideous. Mother was talking about my life like it was a bad episode of "The Real Housewives."

"Ms. Angela, change can be overwhelming, but if you embrace it, each one will get easier," Maria told me.

In that moment, I realized I was in a sad place. A twenty-year-old was giving me life advice for crying out loud. What made it even worse was I knew she had a point.

I took a deep breath and closed my eyes. "Fine. Since I have no clothes and I look like a hag, we might as well go all out."

"I'm sure this is how the people who made 'Waiting to Exhale' and 'How Stella got her Groove Back' started," Maria told me.

I had no idea what she was talking about, but I sat still and let her work.

As the hair dropped down my chest, tears threatened to escape. I wanted to run away, but I had no place to go. The last remnants of my old life were being chopped away, which left me with nothing holding me back from moving forward. That should be exciting for me, but all I felt was fear. I guessed that was better than emptiness. It meant I was feeling again, which was a step in the right direction.

At least I knew that as soon as Maria finished this haircut, I'd be getting food.

Chapter Thirteen

There was nothing worse than shopping for me. Some people considered going to the gym a kind of torture, but I would spend every day there being pushed by one of those overzealous trainers from "The Biggest Loser" if it meant I never had to go shopping again. That might even be the reason my clothes looked like they had come straight out of Michael Jackson's "Thriller" video.

I was not excited about this trip, although Hector and Julio both radiated joy at the idea of going. They weren't happy about my new look, but they were thrilled to visit the big city of Texarkana.

Big cities were terrifying for me, and Texarkana, Texas had over sixty-thousand people. Coming from Sunshine, Texas, that was a population too large to imagine. Even Atlanta, Texas, our closest city, had a population of less than six-thousand people, and when I went there, I always had heart palpitations the whole time. Going to Texarkana for a shopping trip was emotional torture for me, and Mother had planned a full-day experience…

Julio and Hector were at the house by eight am and ready to travel. On the other hand, I wasn't ready until at least eight-thirty. My new haircut threw a wrench in my regular morning routine because I usually put my hair in a bun. On a normal day, it went from wet to up in under thirty seconds, and now I had to fix it. It took me over twenty minutes, and that killed me. According to Maria, we were giving "The Rachel" a revival, just like my life. When had they started naming haircuts? Fortunately for me, we didn't go full blonde, but I did have highlights and volume that actually made me look closer to my thirties.

The makeup project was a whole different issue. After fifteen minutes of attempting to apply foundation, I gave up. I didn't need a thick mask all over my face. It was horrible, and I even had a visible line where the makeup ended around my neck. Maria kept telling me the trick to applying makeup was blending, and she was one-hundred-percent right, but I'd found out this morning that I couldn't blend to save my life. For a southern lady that should be able to do something like this in her sleep, I'd failed miserably.

It made me wonder when I stopped caring about my appearance and let myself go.

"Let's go before I change my mind," I announced as I marched out of my room. My hair was bouncing everywhere, and even though most of my makeup looked terrible and I'd taken it off, I had at least managed to put mascara and lip gloss on.

"Wow, Ms. Angela," Hector said, and he even added a whistle at the end.

"Do that again and you will be failing History next semester," I told him, trying to hide a smile that threatened to come out.

"At the risk of flunking, you look very nice, Ms. Angela," Julio said, as polite as a seventeen-year-old boy could be.

"Thank you, gentlemen," I said as I took a deep breath. I hated compliments, and people observing me. In fact, if I could hide in the shadows, I would probably be much happier.

"Not a bad start at all," Mother said, giving me a close inspection as she moved in a circle around me. She tugged on the bottom of the only skirt she'd left me, and I had a feeling it was only left for this trip.

The forty-five-minute ride to Texarkana was going to be a nightmare.

"Let me grab my keys so we can go," I told the trio.

"No dear, I'm driving," Mother announced as she jingled her keys. "We are not going to the city in your little car. This is a Cadi type of day." With that statement, Mother strolled out of the room doing the best imitation of the "Miss America Walk" I had ever seen.

"Yes! We are riding in the Cadillac," Hector cheered and gave Julio a high-five, then they both ran out of the house after Mother.

"Bonnie, Clyde. You are both in charge of the house. If I'm not back by dusk, call for help because I'm probably dead." I shook my head at myself. I didn't know where this strange habit of giving instructions to my cats anytime I left the house had come from, but I had a feeling it wasn't going anywhere anytime soon.

"Meow," replied Bonnie. I was sure my little girl knew I was in trouble. Clyde stood on the table, looking more than ready to pounce.

"Bite their toes if they don't bring me back, Clyde." Since he was the evil sociopath of my two cats, I knew he'd avenge me if the need ever arose.

"MEOWWW!" he sang.

I didn't care what anyone said, in my heart, I truly believed my cats understood me. If anything, they were the only ones who did. I rushed out the door praying to God I survived this trip.

Mother drove like a bat out of hell all the way to Texarkana. Whoever said old ladies drove slow had never met Mother and her gang. We arrived at the Texarkana Mall in no time. Mother directed us with the skills of an air traffic controller. She sent me to the women's section of Dillard's, and she disappeared with the boys as they headed to J.C. Penney.

Dillard's was bigger than I imagined. They had racks and racks of clothes filled with brands I had never even heard of. With their perfect hair and makeup, the professional sales people looked like they all shopped at the store. This place was too much for me. I was sitting in a dressing room crying when Mother found me two hours later.

"Angela, open the door," she said from the other side of my stall.

I was shaking but managed to pull myself together enough to follow her orders. My mascara was ruined, and I looked like a raccoon.

"Dear, what happened?" Mother took one look at me and the stack of clothes on the floor and moved, pulling wet wipes from her purse and cleaning my face.

"I can't do this," I said, but I struggled to talk between the sobs.

"Why didn't you come and get me?" Mother's voice turned softer and her eyes took inventory of everything.

"I'm forty-five years old, Mother. I should be able to dress myself," I blurted out.

"Oh please, if that was an innate ability, nobody would need personal stylists," she contorted.

I took a deep, shaky breath and pulled myself together. "That is a really good point," I replied and instantly started laughing. It was probably hysteria kicking in.

"Come on, we found some tops we want you to look at before trying them on," Mother said, scooping up as much of the clothing as she could from the floor. "These styles are horrible for you. They'd make you look ancient."

It was sad that my seventy-year-old mother had better taste than me.

Between the two of us, we carried the stack of clothes back to the front of the dressing room and left them with the attendant. The poor girl was giving me such a pitied look that I almost thought she would rush me and give me a hug. Hector and Julio stood by a rack of dresses, examining the pieces that appeared like they just came from a New England pre-school. They wore form-fitting slacks with polo shirts tucked in, and polished shoes. It made them look much older and more mature.

"Wow. Now I'm impressed," I told them both.

"We look like nerds," Hector replied.

"Of course you look like a nerd," Mother replied in a softer voice while she looked at her surroundings. "You are now arms dealers, along with all of us. We need a look that draws the least attention from the authorities as possible."

"Basically, we look like tanned white boys," Julio teased Mother.

"I was thinking bankers or Ivy-League students," I replied, trying not to laugh.

"You both look great, just focus on the money," Mother told the boys and that made them stand up straight again. If that was the uniform for work, they would wear it proudly. "We have work to do, now." Mother pointed at me, and Julio and Hector both got closer.

"The IC collection would look great on Ms. Angela," Julio stated, confidence ringing from his voice. "A conservative line that is still fun, yet stylish too."

I had no idea how he knew that.

"Ms. Angela needs something a little playful. The BB Dakota

brand is definitely a better choice," Hector contradicted his brother.

"How in God's name do you guys know about women's brands and styles?" I blurted.

"When you spend hours listening to your sister ramble about clothes and fashion, you pick up a thing or two," Julio explained.

"Not to mention every trip we took with her involved shopping and being her personal shopping assistants," Hector added, not looking at me but scouting the racks. "We'll be back, Ms. Angela. Don't worry, we got this." Hector and Julio took off, each moving in a different direction.

"Should I be worried I'm going to be dressed by teenage boys?" I asked Mother, and she just smiled proudly.

"Not at all dear. When we are done, you will be breaking hearts everywhere you go," Mother told me as she marched away in a different direction than either of the boys went.

I was left in the middle of the store, holding on to a clothes rack. This was becoming more terrifying by the minute. By the time I decided to run away to the food court, Julio was back with a stack of shirts and pants.

"Here you go," Julio said, pushing me back to my torture chamber. "Go try these on. We need to see what we are working with."

"How do you know my size?" I asked him as I noticed all the clothes were between an eight and a ten.

"Easy. Your mom told us," Julio said, pushing me to the dressing room. "Hurry up. We got tons to do."

That became the drill for the next three hours. One of them found clothes, I tried them on, the group critiqued them, we voted, and then we went to the next pick. I was sure I was going to be sick to my stomach, but after the first round the process became almost fun. They found classic pieces I could match with anything. I got slacks and even two pairs of jeans that could go from casual to dressy pretty easily. If our attempt at arms dealers failed, these three had a career in personal shoppers.

The last part of my day at Dillard's was a little less traumatizing. Mother dragged me to one of those cosmetic stands in the middle of the store. She found the one with the mature sales person instead of the twenty-one-year-old kid with no wrinkles to help me. The sales lady was professional but nurturing and found a line of makeup that was all powder based. She showed me not only what it would look like but how to apply it. The look was really natural, but it made my skin look flawless and polished. Even the boys were impressed.

"Have you considered getting a tan?" Hector asked me on our way to a late lunch or early dinner at Texas Roadhouse.

"Why?" I asked.

"You are pretty pasty, Ms. Angela," Hector said.

Hector needed to work on his bedside manner.

"Hector is right," Mother agreed. "You know, tanned fat looks better than pasty fat."

I had no clue what she was talking about, so I just gave her a perplexed look. "I'm fat?"

"Dear, you are not fat, just flabby," Mother said, not taking her eyes off the road as she maneuvered the three lanes of traffic on the overpass. "As we get older, everything starts to jiggle more."

At least she included herself in that statement.

"Hey, our cousin is a Zumba instructor and just moved back from Miami," Julio said a little too loudly from the back seat.

"You want me to take Zumba?" I had really thought Julio was the nice one in the group.

"Yes and no," Julio rambled.

"Which one is it?" Hector asked, poking his brother in the ribs.

"You should hire him to teach Zumba at the house." Julio dropped the bomb and we all went silent.

"That is not a bad idea at all." Mother was the first one to speak.

"Are you serious?" I asked her, my eyes moving between her and the boys.

"We are opening up a school. This would be great for the kids, and we could even invite the senior community," Mother said, tapping her hands on the steering wheel.

"Are we trying to reduce the senior population by over stimuli?" Zumba for seniors sounded like a cruel game to play.

"Dear, please. Some of those ladies are in better shape than you." Mother was back to throwing low blows. "Besides, this would give us a great excuse for foot traffic around the house."

"Exactly," Julio added.

"Smooth, brother." Hector gave his brother a fist bump.

"I am so slow today." I barely stopped myself from rubbing

my face, but at the last minute I remembered I had makeup on.

"Don't worry dear, we are blaming it on your traumatic shopping experience," Mother told me as she patted my cheeks. I wasn't sure what was worse, the excuse, or the five-year-old treatment.

"I'm on board now, but would your cousin want to do it?" I turned, directing my question at Julio.

"He needs the work, so I don't see why not," Julio said.

"Okay then, give him a call," I told Julio.

"I'll text him," Julio replied as he pulled out his phone. Of course he was going to text. It would be a crime for anyone under the age of twenty five to actually make a sound when communicating with people.

Mother pulled in to the parking lot of Texas Roadhouse and the place looked pretty busy. I wondered if the chain ever had a slow day. The boys were excited and even Mother had a spring in her step. In less than a week, my life hat gotten so much more complicated.

I needed to get home and get a nap, or maybe a shot of scotch. Too bad I threw out all of Todd's supplies when he left.

Chapter Fourteen

It was Monday morning and I finally felt human again. My furry alarm got me up before daylight again. I had no idea why they needed me up, especially since they had an automatic feeder. I guessed if they were going down in flames, they were taking prisoners with them, and that made me their new captive. I chuckled under my breath, even as the idea of getting mad crossed my mind, but really what did I have to be mad about? They'd given me a few hours to myself, to drink my coffee and read my paper in silence. It was ironic, really. When I'd lived alone, I'd hated the quiet and always wanted company. Now, with all the nonstop traffic coming and going from the house, a few hours of peace sounded like heaven.

Bonnie and Clyde had finished their breakfast and were keeping me company on the table as I did a crossword puzzle. I had my CD player in the kitchen playing classic Sinatra, old school style. Nowadays, everyone listened to music online. Heck, they even watched TV shows online. The computer I bought at the pawn shop was in the living room, so technically I could join the in-crowd, but I'd have to learn how to actually use the thing first.

I still needed to find someone who was good with it to help me set up my eBay store and all the other weird stuff we kept doing. According to Minnie and Florence, we needed a Facebook page for all the courses we offered so we could announce it to the city. It was a sad day when the senior community in town was giving me tech lessons.

With a sigh, I grabbed my list of stuff to do online and added Facebook page to it. The list was getting way too long for my taste.

It was probably my fault the list kept growing instead of decreasing. I did nothing all day yesterday. Mother went to church with her gang. The boys went to a Catholic mass with their family and I napped. I organized my closet with all the new clothes and played with the makeup I bought. It finally hit me why I'd given up on makeup so long ago: it was way too damn pricey. Thank God I had the cash, but it still hurt. The satisfying thing was, I now knew how to apply my own makeup again and it looked pretty good.

One day my goal was to look so stunning men would stop in their tracks and wonder where I'd been all their lives.

A hand landed on my shoulder, causing me to scream at the top of my lungs.

"Good morning Angela," Mother said. She had the nerve to chuckle at my reaction, causing a scowl from me. Then she gave me a soft look. "I thought you heard me walking in the kitchen."

"Sorry Mother, I was lost in thought with this puzzle," I told Mother as I lifted the paper for extra emphasis. I would die before I confessed what I'd been daydreaming about.

"Of course, dear," Mother said as she moved to the kitchen area and grabbed coffee. "I was afraid of walking into another feast. You do know we don't exercise enough to eat like that all the time."

"No need to fear. We still have croissants from yesterday, so I decided no need to make more," I told her, pointing to the covered plate on the kitchen island.

"What do you normally eat these things with?" Mother asked as she pulled the cover off the croissants.

"I do jam at times, or Nutella," I told her. "Today I was feeling savory, so I had mine with butter and slices of cheese."

"That sounds good." Mother's eyes searched the kitchen.

"If you are looking for the cheese, is in the fridge," I said, pointing to it just in case she was confused. "You are never up this early, what is going on?"

"Early? Dear, it's already seven," Mother said, her voice a bit on the offended side. She pulled a tray of cheese from the fridge and glanced at me.

Not sure why she was so defensive. Mother was the one person I knew that could stay in bed for twelve hours and still head to bed on time.

"You made that sound like it was supposed to mean something to me," I told her before sipping my coffee.

Mother turned to face me like a pageant queen. "Dear, please tell me you didn't forget. Jesus is coming!"

That was all she said. Had I missed the announcement and

the Apocalypse was upon us?

I looked at Mother in hopes that she would give another hint, but she only stared. I turned to the cats for support, but they both looked at Mother with crooked heads.

Oh, thank the Lord. Even the cats were confused. That made me feel better.

"Mother, was there an announcement made at church yesterday that you forgot to tell me?" If I'd known today was the day I'd meet my maker, I wouldn't have wasted to so much time playing with makeup.

"Not that Jesus," Mother said, shaking her head and layering cheese on top of her croissants.

"You got me then. What Jesus is coming and why?" It was way too early to play fifty questions.

"Zumba Jesus is coming, and remember to pronounce his name is Spanish," Mother said as she made her way towards me at the kitchen table with her plate in one hand and her coffee mug in the other.

"Zumba? Are you talking about Julio and Hector's cousin?" I asked Mother as I realized I'd never learned the cousin's name.

"Yes, and he will be here at eight, so we must get ready quickly," Mother told me as she shoved a large piece of cheese and croissant in her mouth. Mother ate extremely delicate, so watching her shovel food in her mouth without making it a ceremony was unreal.

"Wait, we are starting today?" I asked her when her words finally sank in.

"Of course. The sooner the better," Mother said. "We need to have the word spreading quickly about our classes. I left your yoga clothes in your bathroom so make sure to dress appropriately. The boys should be here soon." She got up from the table and went to the kitchen again.

"Did you two know about this, and that's why you woke me early?" I asked the cats, and they both just stared at me. "I'm taking that as a yes."

There was a conspiracy in my own house and nobody was sharing with me. By the looks of it, I was not going to win. I only wondered who was coming and how many people Mother had shared this news with. I grabbed my coffee and headed towards my room. If Julio and Hector were heading this way to set up, walking around in my PJs was probably not appropriate.

In my bathroom, I found a black pair of yoga pants just like Mother said. She included a hot-pink tank top with it. The clothes were not skin tight, but they were tighter than anything I'd ever owned. At least before my makeover. Now I had a ton of fitting clothes that showed off all the curves I hadn't even known I'd had. I debated not wearing the outfit she'd left out, but I realized I had nothing else that would work with a Zumba class, so by process of elimination, sportswear won.

I put on the clothes, kind of liking the fact that they made me look so much younger. Mother and the boys had talked about Zumba like it was a huge aerobic experience, so I decided to toss my hair up. Maria had said with this hairstyle, I could pull off a messy ponytail and still look good, so I followed her instructions. Sure enough, I ended up with a giant mess, so hopefully that was what she had meant. The last thing I needed was hair sticking to me. I hated that feeling.

I did, however, make sure no stray strands were flying too near my face. The last thing I needed was hair sticking to my forehead, the corners of my eyes, or anywhere else. I hated that feeling.

By the time I stepped out of my room, the place was buzzing with excitement. The Silver Hair Gang was in the house and they were surrounding a man, but I had no idea who since I could only see his back. Julio and Hector were carrying sound equipment to the backyard passed the patio, while Mother was giving a wide smile to the guy surrounded by the gang.

"Angie, dear, you need to meet Jesus," Florence yelled from across the room.

I was pretty sure it was illegal in at least one state for women over the age of sixty to wear spandex in public. The yoga pants the gang, and Mother, were wearing were tighter than mine. They also wore bright shirts, also spandex, but at least they had sleeves.

When Jesus turned and faced me, all the breath went right out of me. He looked like a smooth Ricky Martin, goatee and all. No wonder the gang had swarmed him.

"Hi Ms. Angela, thank you so much for hiring me," Jesus told me, his caramel eyes sparkling as he spoke. The frosted tips on his hair added to his mystique, which was the complete opposite of what Tony's did for him.

"Oh, it's my pleasure Jesus. We are so happy you could be here," I said as I shook his hand.

"Hi Ms. Angela," Julio shouted as he rushed in the living room. "Jesus, where do you want us to put the other speakers?" He pointed toward the backyard where he'd left the speakers.

"Let me take a look at it," Jesus told his cousin, then together they left.

"Wow, he is the instructor?" I asked the group of ladies.

"Oh, trust me, I know," Minnie told me as she glanced around me to get a better a look at our new instructor from my living room window.

"Is that Gertrude?" Ethel asked from behind me.

"Who?" I asked her.

"My nemesis," Ethel replied, almost spitting every word. "We better get out there before she takes the good spot." Ethel, Florence, and Minnie marched outside with a purpose. Mother, on the other hand, seemed to sashay behind them.

"This is getting bigger by the minute," I whispered to Mother.

"This is only the beginning, dear. Just enjoy the ride," Mother told me as she walked out the door, following the rest of the Silver Hair Gang.

Ring. It was the doorbell, so I stopped and glanced at the door like it had sprouted legs. I was so lost. I hadn't been expecting anyone to use the front door, not when the class was in the back. The doorbell rang again. Whoever was out there wasn't giving up easily, so with a sigh I made my way to answer it. It dawned on me that maybe I should get one of the boys for back up, but I decided against it as I grabbed the handle and pulled the door open. My mouth fell open as my eyes landed on James, our county judge.

"Good morning, Angela. I hope this isn't a bad time," James told me as his eyes moved from my head all the way down to my feet in a slow, delicious manner.

It took me a minute to realize he was checking me out. That was when I remembered my skimpy Zumba outfit.

"No, we were just getting ready to start our Zumba class," I told James as I pointed at the backyard.

"You guys do Zumba classes as well?" James asked.

"We do now," I said and just shook my head. "Leave it to Mother to explore her entrepreneur spirit." I must've been spending too much time with Hector because I'd completely lost my filter. Not really the best habit to pick up with the business I was part of.

"That sounds like fun. This town needs new stuff for people to do," James said, shooting me a soft smile.

"How can I help you today, Judge?" I asked, trying to ignore the heat rising to my face.

"Please call me James." His voice had a way of making my knees tremble.

"Sure," I mumbled, losing the ability to form a coherent thought.

"I came to drop off the call list your mother requested," James said, then he handed me a folder.

"What list?" That brought me back to reality.

"Ms. Barbara said you guys will be helping the campaign team by making cold calls," James told me, studying my face with a careful look. "If that isn't the case, please don't feel pressure to do it."

"Of course we're doing it," I said. "I just didn't realize Mother had spoken to you already since we just talked about it this weekend."

How was I supposed to decline when he was right there standing in front of me? That would be so rude, which was probably the reason Mother planned it this way.

"She called Jenny, my campaign manager, Saturday evening with the request," James said, gripping the folder tightly. "I hope you don't mind that I dropped it off. I figured I would save you a trip, especially with your new school commitments," he added as his gaze moved around the room.

"The boys have joined the Zumba class as well," I said. The rumor mill was better than I expected, so I sent a silent thank you to Ethel.

"What you are doing is so noble," James said.

"You give me too much credit. I'm just a woman trying to put her life back together." Not to mention running guns on the side. Definitely nothing noble about that. I took a deep breath and smiled. "I should take that from you. You probably have a lot going on." I stretched out my hand and waited for James to hand me the folder.

"Thank you again, Angela. Your support means a lot to me." James planted the folder in my extended hand.

I was afraid to speak since I was sure my voice would just

crack. All I did was grin like a fool, and when he turned to leave, I waved.

Killing Mother had just moved to the top of my list.

I stood in the doorway and watched James disappear into his car and then out of my driveway. When I closed my door, Latin music blared from the backyard, so I inched that way, dropping the folder on the coffee table as I went. Before I went out the back door, I glanced through the window. It was a traumatic sight. Over ten senior ladies were bouncing to at least ten different beats. Not one of them were doing anything remotely similar to what Jesus did.

This was going to be painful, but I put on a brave face and headed outside.

Chapter Fifteen

$\mathcal{B}$y the time four o'clock rolled around, I was feeling good. It was the first time in months, maybe even years, that I'd felt this cheerful. According to Jesus, exercise released dopamine into the body and dopamine was the "feel good hormone." Maybe it was the hormone, but it could've been the Latin music, or even the great lunch that came after the Zumba class. Either way, I was high on happiness.

After lunch, I made my way to every pawn shop in Cass County. According to Dad's journals, he purchased carrying cases, holsters, and other supplies from all over the area. His actual guns, though, he got from only two dealers. One was Joe, but the other was an outsider—one I'd never met. The less people that had direct contact with his money, the better, at least according to Dad. I trusted his logic and decided having another source to buy arms wouldn't hurt.

I had borrowed Minnie's Lincoln for this trip. It was huge and had plenty of space to carry everything. I'd purchased enough cases for our next delivery, plus I added some extras. With business out of the way, I made a trip to Walmart in Atlanta for groceries and household items. It was the first chance I'd had to stock up on stuff without feeling guilty. Money was no longer an option, so with nothing holding me back, I actually allowed myself to splurge a little by purchasing a few CDs and movies.

Since Mother had gone off to pick up some extra guns that she'd tucked away in her storage unit, I planned to spend my evening cleaning and inspecting. Unfortunately, when I pulled up to my street, firetrucks and police cars surrounded my house.

Shock held me hostage for a moment, but when it released me, I stared at the purse that housed my cell phone. It had been there the whole time. Why hadn't anyone called me. Panic settled in my chest, making it hard to breathe. I hoped everyone was okay.

With a bunch of officers around, speeding down my street didn't seem like the best option. Instead, I passed my house and pulled in the first empty space on the block.

After parking the car, I grabbed a couple of grocery bags, making sure to make myself look as helpless as possible. I left the gun cases in the car. The last thing I needed was to draw attention to myself. The Smith and Wesson was inside my bag, but this was Texas and everyone carried a concealed gun with them. Nothing looked out of order. The place did not look burned down or in need of this much attention.

"Good afternoon, Officer," I said as soft and polite as possible.

"Good afternoon, Ms. Angela. How are you?" It was Deputy Sheriff Miller who turned to face me.

Miller was only a few years younger than me, but he always talked to me like I was his mother. It was annoying, especially since Miller was a handsome brunette with high cheek bones and a perfect complexion.

"It was pretty good until now. What is going on in my house?" I asked Miller, pointing toward the scene of the crime.

"I'm all about equality, but it might not be the best idea to leave a couple of teenagers, a bunch of old ladies, and a couple cats in charge of cooking," Miller said, as if that was supposed to mean something. He must have noticed my confused look because he added, "They are bound to break something."

"Of course, Deputy Sheriff. I'll make sure it doesn't happen again," I replied, doing my best to sound embarrassed and remorseful.

"Good," Miller replied, sticking his chest out like he actually had accomplished something.

"All clear," one of the firefighters yelled at Miller as he went back to his fire truck.

"Ms. Angela, it looks like you can get in your house now," Miller told me, gesturing to the house. "Just remember to keep an eye on that group. They should not be allowed to cook or grill unsupervised." Miller tilted his hat and took off.

This couldn't be good. I had no idea what to expect, but standing outside was not going to help anyone, including me. I took a deep breath and forced myself to walk. Images of battle fields and destruction filled my head. Nothing of the sort faced me when I got in. The house was painfully boring, as usual. I was adding painting the house to the boys' list of things to do.

"Bonnie, Clyde, Mother," I called. "You guys in here?" It felt odd coming in from the front door. Usually I entered the house from the garage.

"I'm glad that you checked on the cats before your own mother," Mother told me as she came into the living room from the kitchen.

"Hey, I figured if the cats were missing, the situation was worse than I expected," I told her, dropping my bags on the coffee table. "What is going on? You have firetrucks, police cars, and every volunteer in the entire town outside the house."

"Angie, sweetie, we had a situation." Minnie came in right behind Mother, sporting her signature red lips that were shining brighter than Rudolph's nose.

"Ms. Angela, they tried to scare us away, but we held our ground," Hector told me as he came in from the backyard.

The boys and the Silver Hair Gang came from every direction, which made it a little hard to keep up with everything they were saying.

"Everyone, stop!" I yelled at the group. "I only need one person to explain what is going on, and how about we start from the beginning." I crossed my arms over my chest and backed up, giving me the opportunity to glance at each of them as I waited for a volunteer.

"I'll do it," Ethel offered. "But you are not going to like it. Also, I'm going to need you to promise not to kill the messenger."

This was worse than Deputy Miller's warning.

I let out a long sigh. "I think someone a little less dramatic is needed." My eyes roamed the room again.

"Hey, I'm offended." Ethel's right hand went over her heart.

"You will get over it. Just the facts, if you please. None of that color commentating." My happy mood had vanished. Now I wanted nothing more than to get to the bottom of this.

"Fine," Ethel said and took a look around the room before starting. "We were paid a visit by Billy's gang and they wanted double the weapons you are giving Tony next week. They threatened to take some of us as hostages to make you cooperate. Bonnie and Clyde intervened, giving us time to set off the fire alarm and call for help. Billy left, but we have a meeting tomorrow at Buckhorn Creek to discuss delivery."

"What?" I had no other words, and nobody else was saying a word. Probably because I had told them only one of them could talk, but either way, I needed to know more. I hadn't been gone that long, had I?

"You said just the facts, and no color-commentating." Ethel smirked.

I didn't find little Ms. Smarty Pants very funny in that moment.

"Fine," I said as I stepped to the sofa and took a seat. Good thing I'd made it. My legs felt pretty weak. "Give me enough color to make sense of the facts, then, because I'm totally lost. What is going on? Who is Billy?"

"It seems Tony has a rival gang that is supplying guns to the other side," Mother jumped in. "They heard about your deal with Tony and they want in."

"Can we just sell guns to both sides?" Hector asked us.

"The government does all the time," I answered him. "That is not the problem. The fact that they came to our house and threatened us is the issue. They are definitely not the type of people we want to work with. We'd have to watch our backs forever." I was not happy another gang knew about us.

"I fear we're already in that boat," Florence added. "They don't seem like the type to take no for an answer. Unless you are planning to teach them a lesson, we might be stuck with them."

I didn't want to admit it, but Florence had a point.

"How about we face one issue at a time?" I asked the group. "First is this meeting. What is that all about?"

"Billy wants to present his proposal to us, and 'the sooner the better.' His words, not mine" Julio piped in.

"Who picked the Buckhorn Creek at Lake O' the Pines Dan as the meeting place?" Next time I'd have to ask for more color. The facts they'd given me were still pretty muddy. I feared I'd never understand at this rate.

"We needed to get them out of the house before the cops got here," Ethel said. "Last thing we wanted was to be associated with them in any way. And, as for the lake, it's always been a great place to get rid of a body, just in case things to get messy." Her tone came out as all business, and more than serious.

"Ethel is right, we need the home turf advantage without having them here," Minnie supplied.

If I'd wondered how deadly Mother's gang really was, I had my answer. I had a feeling the ladies in front of me wouldn't think twice about shooting someone just for pissing them off.

"I don't like any of this, but the meeting is necessary," I told the group. "What time is the meeting with them?"

"Seven O'clock, right after sunrise," Mother told me. "We need to be on the road by six thirty."

"We?" I asked as my gaze travelled the length of the room. "Who do you think is coming?" Have they lost their minds? That was a silly question. Of course they had.

"Angie dear, we are all going," Florence told me as she fixed her fifties pin-up peach dress. She did look fabulous today.

"This is way too dangerous for you guys. I'll go by myself," I announced like I was in charge.

"You are not a going alone," Mother corrected.

"This is too dangerous," I counteracted.

"Exactly the reason you are not going alone," Ethel said, and I could tell the rest of the Silver Hair Gang were getting ready to fight my argument all night long.

"I'm not going to win this, am I?" I asked before heading down that path.

"Not at all," Minnie said, "Just breathe and relax. We got this. This is a family affair and those dicks just messed with the wrong family," she said as she moved over to my chair.

"Minnie, vocabulary," I said as my mouth dropped open. I couldn't believe she'd said that.

"Angela, I'm too old to give a damn who I offend anymore," Minnie said as she ran her fingers through her hair.

"While we are discussing organizing tomorrow's events, remember at seven we'll be making our phone calls," Mother told us. "Bring your phones and be prepared to call the world. The judge has even agreed to come out and help with the first few calls."

"What? Why?" I blurted out before I could think.

"It seems normally people do the phone bank from his campaign location, so he feels guilty we are using our own space," Mother explained. "To help us out, James and Jenny will be joining us for calling. Isn't he sweet?" Droopy smiles from the Silver Hair gang filled the room. They were definitely some of James's biggest fans. For me, in the grand scheme of things, I'd rather face the angry gang members than risk having alone time with James.

"Sounds like tomorrow is going to be busy," I told the group. "I'm assuming we don't really have dinner ready?" I looked around and all I got were head shakes. "That's what I figured. Julio, Hector, can you please pull the Lincoln closer to the house and unload everything." I gave the boys the keys to the car and they raced out the door.

"You are taking this very well," Mother told me.

"We don't have much of a choice, do we?" I replied.

"We could always be freaking out," Florence said in a mocking voice.

"Too late for that," I told them. "Freaking out is out of the question. Let's focus on making the most of the day. Did you get all the weapons?"

"Everything is in Barbara's room," Minnie said like a school girl at the prom.

"It's time for us to get busy cleaning," I told the ladies. "Half of us can get dinner ready, and everyone else is on gun detail. Pick whatever you prefer."

I had spent too many restless nights worrying about all my failures. Things never turned out as horrible as I imagined. I was not planning to do that anymore. If I was to die the next day, then I would do it with a full belly. It was time to focus on the things I could control. The rest God could figure out. I headed towards my room to change into my new jeans and a shirt so I could start cleaning guns.

Chapter Sixteen

𝒢t was no surprise that I couldn't sleep that night. In front of everyone, I could pretend to be brave and strong. I had years of practice faking it, pretending I was happy and life was great when really it was a pile of crap. At night, when I was alone in my bed, it was a different story. Sometimes, I even thought the walls were closing in on me. A lot of times, I'd lay down crying, feeling sorry for myself, and then the self-loathing would take over, making me lose myself in pain and suffering.

This night was different. The longer I laid awake, the angrier I became. A group of punks came into my house and threatened my friends and family. I was tired of being told what I was and was not going to do. I'd had enough, and I did not feel like dancing to anyone else's drum. For some strange reason, I wasn't sure if my anger was directed towards the new gang, or if it was because Todd had left me and found happiness with Barbie, or Sunshine, Texas, for putting me in a box.

None of it really mattered, but by the time five came around, I was madder than ever and ready for war.

I dressed in a pair of Capri pants, a cardigan, and boots—definitely not my usual outfit, but I wasn't really feeling like my usual self. The pity had disappeared and in its place was a holy determination I hadn't felt since I was a teenager. No idea how this day was going to play out, but we had plenty of bullets for an old-fashioned shoot out.

Bonnie and Clyde were waiting by the bedroom door when I emerged from the bathroom.

"Meow," screamed Clyde.

"Mommy is okay, honey." I rubbed his forehead and he purred. "Mommy is going to deal with a few wild little boys, but I got this." I had no idea what the plan would be, but I knew there'd be one. Eventually.

Mother was ready to go at a quarter before six. A battle with punks seemed to get everyone up and ready early.

"Now this is a surprise," I told Mother.

"Couldn't sleep," she replied.

"That makes two of us," I admitted on my way to the coffee. "Hope you don't mind if we skip breakfast today?" I asked.

"That's a great plan," Mother concurred. "Last thing we need is to get sick before war. Are you ready for this?" She took a sip of her coffee after she spoke.

"I doubt Jesus was ready to die, and trust me when I tell you I'm not ready either," I said, taking my first sip of life. "But we will not be bullied around. Let's go and see what they have to offer."

"The girls are on their way," Mother told me. "Julio and Hector are ready; they just need a text." I was impressed. She'd checked on everyone.

"As soon as they get here, we leave," I told her on my way to the knife drawer. I pulled out a Glock G29 and tucked it in the back of my Capri pants. "What are you carrying, Mother?"

"My Beretta, dear, what else?" That was Mother's weapon of choice. I knew that but just wanted to confirm she was packing.

"Do you have enough ammo?" I was doing last minute checks for myself.

"We are taking the Cadi, so trust me, dear, we got plenty." Even though Mother wasn't fazed by my questions, I could tell she was deep in thought. It made me wonder what those thoughts might be, but I couldn't bring myself to ask.

Beep. It was Mother's phone.

There was no need for words. When Mother stood and grabbed her purse, I followed behind her with my Smith and Wesson tucked inside my own bag.

Next time, I was going to veto for location, like this lake. Mother was driving like we were heading to a picnic, slowly and without a care in the world. That way she would not attract any attention from the law. Not that it mattered since the roads were empty, other than us. Minnie was driving her Lincoln and Hector rode shotgun with her. Florence and Ethel were driving another Cadi with Julio in the back. If we ever got pulled over, I had no clue what the officers would think of our little crew. Although it might be a good laugh just to see their faces.

I watched Mother maneuver the curves of Lake O' the Pines Dan like a pro. She knew exactly where Buckhorn Creek Overlook Point was located. It was probably a blessing she was driving because I was totally lost. In the darkness before dawn, the place looked creepy and intimating.

Mother found a spot overlooking the water and parked the Cadi. She picked her location very strategically, leaving a great view to all directions and no way for anyone to sneak up behind us. Curiosity was kicking in and I wanted to know what kind of wild life the Silver Hair Gang had back in the day.

Right at seven, two Ford F-150s pulled up to our location. At least they were punctual, but I didn't know if that was a good sign or not. We waited until the trucks were parked and watched as the passengers climbed out.

"Ready, dear?" Mother asked me.

"As ready as I'm going to be," I replied and slowly climbed out of the Cadi.

Our little meeting looked like something out of a movie. We walked to the mid-point of each vehicle and stopped about five feet away from each other. I had transferred the Smith and Wesson to my boot and left the purse in the car. Four tall young men faced us. Two in front and the other two a few steps behind them. I'd expected to find four Latin guys conducting the deal, but instead the four Caucasians stood in front of me. Maybe they were from the government after all.

"You must be the Cat Lady?" a blond guy with grey eyes said. He was probably Billy, the leader. "I was expecting someone different."

"So was I," I replied without any emotions. "You must be Billy." He only raised an eyebrow in response. He was an arrogant little brat. "I don't have all day, so get to it. What do you want?" I shot out, tapping my foot against the ground.

"Wow, what happened to southern hospitality?" Billy asked and at that moment I realized he didn't have an accent. Not even a little bit. His speech was the clearest I'd ever heard, the type one only learned at school.

"Dear, that went out the door the moment you went to my house and threatened my family." I made sure to make my accent as thick as possible.

"That is a shame," Billy said, but his words didn't match his tone. There was nothing remorseful about him. "We were hoping to start over. You probably don't have the right opinion of us." He tried to smile at me but even that came across as fake.

"What impression should we have of you?" I asked, even as I wondered how long this little game would last.

"We are businessmen searching for a good deal," Billy said as he pointed at his buddies. "We heard the Carters were back in business and we want in." I had years of practice controlling my facial expressions, so even though his statement might have rattled me a little, I didn't show it. Also, I preferred to continue thinking of them as Tony's rival gang.

"That sounds like a rumor to me," I told Billy. "What do you think, Mother?" I turned, almost in slow motion, towards Mother.

"Honey, you know how the rumor mill in Sunshine works," Mother replied, also laying on her southern accent as thick as she could. It made sense. I'd learned the trick from her, so I had a feeling she'd figure out what I was trying to do.

"Ladies, this is not the time to play dumb," Billy told us and snapped his fingers. The two thugs in the back both produced two revolvers.

Unfortunately for Billy, our group came with a bit more fire power. Julio had an M16 pointed at the group from the sunroof of the Cadi. Hector and Ethel were both packing Remington's and stood right outside of the group to make sure we didn't get shot by accident. Friendly fire still killed people. Minnie and Florence carried shotguns and were inside. If all hell broke loose, they were to wipe everyone out and ask questions later. There was nothing scarier than a group of old ladies fully packed and pointing deadly weapons at you.

I gave the boys a minute to take inventory of our side before talking. "I agree." I plastered my own fake smile on my face. "This is not the time to play dumb, so let's get to the point. What do you want?"

Billy gave his boy a hand signal and they lowered their weapons. Too bad our side didn't follow suit. "I want double what you're giving Tony and his boys, and I want it by next Monday."

"Wow, that's it?" I asked Billy, crossing my arms. "Why should we do this?" This negotiation seemed a little one sided.

"Simple, my dear Cat Lady," Billy said, licking his lips. I wanted to slap the arrogance out of him. "If you don't, we will contact the Feds and turn you in. It would be a shame for the citizens of Sunshine and Cass County to find out they have deadly criminals in their mists. We can also pin a few more arms deliveries to the Carter family, ones that were involved in awful crimes."

Billy was good, I'd give him that. He smirked as he waited for my response. I let him wait a little bit, too.

"Well sounds like we have ourselves a deal," I told him. Mother tensed beside me. When I turned to look at her, her back was straight stiff, but she kept her mouth shut. I turned back to Billy. "Next Monday it is, same time and place." Negotiations were over, so I turned to leave.

"If you betray us, it will not be pretty for you," Billy said in a soft voice.

"Bring cash only, three hundred per item and don't be late," I replied in a no-nonsense tone. "Your guns will be here. This is the last time the Carters will do business with you, dear. Next time you contact us, you will find a 9mm between your eyes. Is that clear?" I stopped and looked directly at Billy. I had never killed a person in my life, but I was willing to make an exception with this one.

"Deal, Cat Lady." After a wicked grin, Billy left.

What a brat. Always had to have the last word.

I gave our team a head nod and everyone got in their vehicles, except Julio. He stayed where he was, his gun pointed on the four thugs and their trucks until they drove away. I climbed in the Cadi with Mother and we waited until the trucks disappeared before speaking.

"Angela, this is not going to end," Mother said as she started the car.

"I know, Mother, but we just bought ourselves some time," I told her. "We need a plan to get rid of them once and for all, but declining them now was not an option," I said as I watched her drive slowly down the path.

"I'm not sure if I should be mad at your father or not," Mother said in a gentle voice.

"Dad is gone, Mother, and he provided us a really good life,"

I told her, staring out the window. "If you want to be mad at somebody, be mad at me for opening this life back up." I hesitated to face her because I was afraid of what she would say, but I could still hear her whether I looked at her or not.

"I couldn't be mad at you, dear," Mother said, but she didn't take her eyes of the road. "I would be a hypocrite for being happy about the money and mad about the consequences that come with this life. I also know how hard things have been for you recently. I was helpless to do anything about it. I'm willing to die for you now."

"Mother," I half-shouted, but my voice broke from the emotion in that one word. I didn't know if I wanted to hug her or yell at her. She was not a woman to talk about her feelings, so this was huge for her. "Let's try to make sure nobody dies. As long as we make it, everything will be just fine." I reached over to squeeze her hand.

"We will think of something," Mother told me, then she winked at me. "Text the girls, tell them we are heading to the city for breakfast."

I gave Mother a wide-eyed stare. "Breakfast in Texarkana on a Tuesday?" Texarkana was a weekend trip for most people in Sunshine, so heading there on a Tuesday was definitely living on the wild side.

"I'm craving Cracker Barrel," Mother said, and that was the only answer I needed to hear.

"Breakfast it is," I replied, holding in the chuckle threatening to escape.

I took my phone out and texted the passengers in both vehicles. The idea of breakfast in Texarkana got everyone excited. Not to mention, it gave us a place to talk where nobody knew us. For a person who enjoyed the small-town life, I'd been spending quite a bit of time making crazy trips right outside my comfort zone.

Now we just needed a plan to get rid of Billy and his boy band. Then everything would be perfect.

Chapter Seventeen

Getting the Silver Hair Gang out of Texarkana was like trying to pull a kid out of Disney. We went to every weird antique shop they'd ever heard of and stopped by every second hand store in the city. No idea why, because none of them purchased a single item. Four women who owned everything they'd ever desired had no need to go shopping. This was just entertainment, but only for them. It was still torture for me.

I finally dragged them away after lunch. That was after reminding them we had a phone bank to conduct at seven and that the boys needed to start their school work. Mentioning school had Hector complaining and Julio cheering. The surprise reaction came from Minnie and Florence. Back in their youth, they were both school teachers, so they were more than ready to help with the boys.

Ethel had established a teaching schedule for everyone and assigned subjects. Somehow, I'd gotten stuck with history. It had been twenty years since I picked up a history book, in any form or capacity. I loved the History Channel, but I was sure that didn't qualify me to be a teacher on the subject. My protests were ignored, and even Hector thought I would do a great job. This school idea was turning into a lot more work for me than I'd expected.

My session was Friday morning, so that gave me two days to come up with an actual lesson plan. Ethel took the first session, math, and it started this afternoon before the phone bank. She had prepared a small quiz for the boys to gage their level of knowledge. When she had the time to develop a quiz was beyond me. I was barely wrapping my mind around the fact that we were going to run a school, and Ethel already had testing materials.

We arrived at my house a little after two and everyone scattered with plans to meet back at the house to start lessons and curriculum development. I was able to get a pass on the prepping time to research Dad's journal. If Billy knew about my dad's clandestine life, I was hoping Dad had known about his. Normally, I would change into house clothes, but this time I gave up that idea. If people were coming over later, I needed to look presentable.

I gave the cats a quick treat and headed straight for the bunker.

At six forty-five, I headed back to the house. I had four notebooks that my dad had documented from five years ago. It appeared the business had been booming thanks to a small militia group from Missouri. Dad had started providing arms to a group that was taking on a drug cartel. Being the visionary business owner he was, Dad had started providing guns to the cartel as well. Word spread and business had been coming from everywhere.

"Angela, are you hungry?" Mother asked when I entered the house from the patio.

"Food?" Didn't we just eat? The house smelled of tamales, quesadillas, and Spanish rice. I was definitely not used to eating this much in one day, but my stomach, being the traitor that she was, grumbled at the smell of food.

"Your stomach is saying something different," Minnie said as she walked from the kitchen with a plate.

"I swear I'm not really that hungry," I tried to explain. "It's probably just because everything smells amazing. Where did you get the food from?" I asked the ladies as I made my way to the kitchen.

The kitchen was packed with warming trays. Julio, Hector, and even Maria were helping serve food. Florence and Ethel were passing plates around, along with two young ladies I had never met before. One of the girls had spiky grey hair. That fashion trend still alluded me. Why would anyone purposely dye their hair grey? The other one was not doing any better. She had blue highlights.

"Hi, Ms. Angela, can we make you a plate?" Maria asked, waving an empty paper plate around.

"Make her something small, sweetie. She isn't too hungry," Minnie told Maria from behind me. I was starting to think this was a conspiracy against me.

"Here you go, Ms. Angela." Julio handed me a large glass filled with some kind of white substance. "It's Horchata, freshly made."

Horchata was a Mexican drink made of rice. I took one sip and it was delicious. I only knew one person who made Horchata this good, and that was Ana, the boys' mom.

"How did you convince your mother to cook all this?" I took a stab and asked Julio.

"Mrs. Barbara asked Mom to cater the phone bank," Maria answered as she handed me a plate.

"Are we expecting more people? This is a lot of food." We had enough to feed at least thirty people.

"Jenny and the judge are bringing four more people with them," the young lady with blue hair told me.

"They are bringing more chairs as well," the grey-haired one said. "When your mother heard that our other call group couldn't meet, she offered for us to join you here. You ladies are so nice," the young girl said as she bounced off to the living room.

"I heard you had cats. Where are they?" the blue-haired girl asked me.

I had a feeling the whole county knew I was the crazy cat lady.

"That is a really good question, dear," I responded, looking around the kitchen for my cats. "I left them in the kitchen earlier today." It didn't take me long to find them. They were hiding on the top of the kitchen cabinets, glaring down at the group. I pointed at my kids and the young lady squealed with excitement.

"They are so cute," she said as she moved in their direction and reached a hand towards them. She was lucky they were so high up, otherwise little blue tip would be missing a finger. Clyde was not the one to be touched without his permission.

"I recommend not touching them," I told her and grabbed my plate from Maria, who was trying hard not to laugh.

"Thank you, Maria, and please give my thanks to your mother," I told her.

"She is excited to help," Maria told me. "Besides, your mother paid very well for everything."

"Mother always pays well for things she enjoys," I told Maria.

"Ms. Angela, are you okay with me staying to help?" Maria

asked as she pulled out her phone.

"Of course, sweetie, you don't have to ask." I had to admit, Ana had the most polite kids on the planet. Even Hector, with his little defiant streak, was very well mannered.

I reached the living room in time for the doorbell to ring. Florence came running from behind me to open the door. I had never seen a person move so fast in heels and a dress. I wasn't sure why nobody ever commented on Florence's dresses the way they did mine. Then again, Florence looked like a fifties Hollywood star every day and I looked like I was working in the coal mines. I nixed the idea of ever asking that question out loud.

"Good evening, Judge James, come in," Florence announced a lot louder than required.

A petite lady, maybe in her thirties, followed James. She had shoulder-length black hair and a no-nonsense kind of look that matched the sharp haircut she wore. Right behind her were three older ladies and a gentleman, all in their late fifties or sixties.

"Thank you, Ms. Florence. We are so grateful for the invitation," James told Florence in that sexy voice that made women blush. Or maybe it just made me blush. I wasn't sure.

It was rude to listen to other people's conversations, so I walked to the furthest part of the living room. As soon as all the ladies were inside, James brought folding chairs in. Julio was already at the door helping with the process. If I didn't know any better, I would have sworn they had done this before. Chairs were arranged against the wall and our new guests were offered plates of food. Mother was playing host, so all I had to do was wave every now and then from my corner. Go Mother!

After everyone was served and introductions were made, everyone found a chair. The no-nonsense lady turned out to be Jenny, and she was as efficient as her look suggested. Within five minutes, she had distributed phone scripts to everyone, explained the process, and even role played how to properly conduct a call with Julio. I tried to remember everything she had said, but I struggled just memorizing all the names of the new arrivals.

The list included five hundred numbers, and based on Ethel's calculations, we each had to make thirty-one calls. Our phone bank was only scheduled until eight. Jenny said they tried to avoid making calls after that since a lot of their contingencies were heading to bed after eight. Ethel believed that shouldn't be a problem if we kept the calls to under a minute. That all sounded great in theory, but after dealing with people all these years, I'd learned plans never went quite as expected.

My suspicions were confirmed when my first call lasted seven minutes. I managed to get one of my old elementary teachers that was still alive. We talked about everything and I struggled to get off the phone with her. By the time I was done with my first three, Julio and Hector had talked to fifteen each. I was failing at the call center and decided to get a refill of Horchata. Bonnie and Clyde were still hiding and watching me from the top of the cabinets they'd perched on.

"You are doing great, you know," James said from behind me.

After I grabbed the Horchata from the fridge, I turned around. "I managed to have the longest calls out of everyone."

"It's not about how many people you call. It's about how many you connect with. How many will come to the election and vote because you made that connection," James explained. "Your three and their family will be at the election just because you called them."

"You give me too much credit," I told him as I took a sip of Horchata. I grabbed a glass from the cabinet and poured him one. James hadn't asked, but it felt rude drinking in front of him.

"Thank you," he said in a soft voice as he took the glass from me. "You care about people and you listen to their concerns. That is something you can't fake, and people connect with that." He took a sip of his Horchata and waited for my response.

"Thank you, but now you are just being nice," I said, and I could feel the heat rising in my cheeks. I had no idea why he had this effect on me. "We are glad to help."

"You are all in trouble," James said, pointing at our little crew. "You guys are too efficient. Jenny will never let you go, especially since you fed people without being asked."

I looked in the direction of the living room and found Jenny beaming from ear to ear. "Food was Mother's idea, of course." I wished I could take the credit, but entertaining crowds was her superpower.

"You still agreed to host at your house, so thank you," James told me, and he gave me a smile that made his eyes sparkle.

I stared for way too long, and I had to force myself to look away before I fell right into those sparkling eyes. Even though my glass was still half full, I turned and dumped it right in the sink just to have a reason to look somewhere else.

"Let me go call my next three lucky winners," I told James. So afraid of touching him, I plastered myself against the wall as I moved past him. If we touched, I knew I'd go up in flames and I had no time for that.

"You will do great," James replied. He followed behind me as we made our way to the living room. I glanced at his cup. Smart man, keeping his drink. I hadn't been so smart.

The remaining twenty-five minutes making calls went fast. I managed to contact seven more people, making five more calls that had disconnected numbers. My numbers weren't even close to Julio's or Hector's, but at least I'd managed to hit double digits. By the time we concluded our session, we only had about one hundred numbers left on the page, a fact that excited Jenny. She claimed rookies never got those kinds of numbers. Needless to say, Jenny and Mother made arrangements for the next campaign project, while Maria and Minnie handed to-go containers to everyone who left.

Julio and Hector helped the older group get in their van, while James carried the chairs back. I was stuck with Ethel, helping her tally up the list of wrong numbers, the ones we left messages to, and the ones we needed to call back. Florence had made friends with some of the other ladies, so she'd accompanied them out to the van. I knew very little about campaign management, but it looked like a great success.

"Angela," James had come back in the house. I quickly stood up while Ethel continued her inventory.

I shot to my feet clumsily, wiping my hands down the front of my outfit. "Do you need anything?" I stuttered, unsure what else to say.

"No, I'm good," James said with one of those breathtaking smiles of his.

"That's what they all say," Ethel said from her chair, which made James turn a bright shade of red. I kept my eyes trained on anything but her while pretending I hadn't heard her.

"I just wanted to thank you again," James trailed off. His gaze fell to the floor. "And I hope to see you again soon," he mumbled, and it was so hard to hear him I thought maybe he hadn't meant to say those words.

"It was our pleasure," I said as I tucked a strand of hair behind my ear.

"You've been doing that all night," James mentioned and adjusted the piece of hair I'd missed.

"New cut and I'm still not used to it," I admitted.

"It looks great," James said.

"It was all Maria. She did it," I said, trying to get the attention off me. I'd never been comfortable accepting compliments.

"She does look great, right?" Ethel said from her seat.

I gave her my meanest glare, but she just ignored it.

"She always does," James said.

Not for the first time, I wondered if I could find a rock big enough to hide under.

Ethel giggled from her chair.

"James, we're ready," Jenny yelled from the door.

"Good night, Ms. Ethel, Angela," James said with a nod of his head towards each of us.

I had no words, so I just waved, but as soon as he turned, I collapsed in my chair.

"Saved by the Gestapo," Ethel teased me.

"You are ruthless," I told her.

"Maybe, but you are slow," Ethel told me. "You are now a lethal business woman. Grow a pair and go for it." She poked me in the leg, and I decided that was my cue to run away.

I did not need dating advice from the Silver Hair Gang. I decided to head to the kitchen to help clean up, but between Mother and Maria, everything was done. In fact, when I came in, Mother was speaking to Maria, who was taking notes on whatever she was dictating. Or scheming. Probably the latter.

"What are you two planning?" I asked them once I reached the kitchen's island.

"Mrs. Barbara is going to offer brunch as part of the registration fee for the Zumba classes," Maria said, waving her list at me.

"Really?" That was a really good idea.

"We are raising the price to ten dollars, which will include the food," Mother explained. "If we can get fifty people here, we can make it worth the trouble for Jesus and help him out."

"We do have room in the backyard," I told Mother. "What do I need to do?"

"You are in charge of covering the food expenses until we start making money," Mother announced. "About two hundred will cover Wednesday and Friday." I was not liking this plan now.

"That would be plenty," Maria said with a wide grin.

"Let me get my purse," I told Maria with a sigh.

"Don't worry, Ms. Angela, you can pay me tomorrow," Maria said. "I'll make sure to get you a receipt. Thank you for letting us come tonight. We had a great time." Before I had a chance to say a word, Maria's arms were around me. She was a hugger, for sure, which made me a little uncomfortable, but I was getting used to it.

In fact, I even hugged her back. "I'm glad you guys came," I told her, and it surprised me how much I meant every word.

"We are leaving the left overs here if that's okay," Maria said. "That way we can give it to some of the seniors that come to class tomorrow."

"That is a really good idea," I told Maria.

She beamed. "Thanks. Well, I am calling it a day. Good night," Maria said as she headed out the kitchen door.

"What do you think if…" Mother started.

"Don't even think about it," I interrupted.

"You don't know what I was going to say," Mother placed her hand over her heart, faking shock.

"I don't need to," I told her. "We have too much going on to add another project. Let's fix problem number one before adding more to our plate, okay?" I tapped my foot on the floor as I waited for her reply.

"Fine, for now," Mother agreed.

I had a feeling whatever she was thinking would probably be another great idea. She'd been flooded with them lately. But we had no time for anymore projects, at least not at the moment.

"I'm heading to bed, unless you need my help here?" I could see there wasn't much for me to do, but my manners made me ask.

"No dear, the girls and I are planning to play Canasta. Get some rest."

I guessed Mother was intending to have a long night.

I said my good nights to everyone else and headed to my room. Bonnie and Clyde followed right behind me after the room cleared out. I wanted a bath, and then I wanted sleep. Too much had gone on today and I needed a break from people. The madness could commence tomorrow. For tonight, it was time for a little *me* time.

Chapter Eighteen

It was almost six-thirty when I crawled out of bed, and my furry alarms hadn't woken me. That worried me. As I made my way through my room, the cats were nowhere to be found, so as quiet as I could, I relocated to the living room. Nobody was there, but I smelled the salty goodness of bacon, so I followed the scent into the kitchen, finding my cats eating with Mother.

"Good morning," I told the trio with my hands on my hips. They all froze in their spots. Somehow all three looked like kids caught with their hands in the cookie jar, or the bacon pan to be more precise.

"Good morning dear. Hungry?" Mother asked, handing me a piece of bacon.

I took the bacon. "What are you doing up?"

"You are not the only one who can get up and make breakfast," Mother said as she stood and stepped to the coffee pot, pouring me a cup.

"You couldn't sleep, could you?" I asked, not believing the breakfast act for a second.

"I ate too much last night and had heartburn," said Mother.

"So you decided to make more food?" That was a different way to tackle that issue.

Mother shrugged. "I couldn't go back to sleep." She paced around the kitchen until she stopped at the small dining table. "I actually found those books you brought with you last night and started reading them." I squinted, finding Mother had Dad's notebooks in her arms. "I feel like I didn't know a thing about your dad." She leaned against the island, still holding the notebooks.

"Dad had a lot of secrets, Mother," I said, realizing how true it really was. "A lot of them were to keep us safe."

"That's the problem," Mother said, tears brimming in her

eyes. "He carried the weight of this house all alone and never once complained. He still had a full-time job." I wasn't sure where Mother was going with this conversation when she reached for my hand. "Promise me you won't do the same."

I was a little stunned. Mother held my hand so tight and I had no idea what to say in response to her words, so I said the first thing that came to me. "Mother, I'm not hiding anything."

"You are so much like your dad," Mother said, her voice cracking. "You are willing to sacrifice your whole life for the people you love. Stop that!" she yelled. "You are not alone. Don't ever think you are. Please, promise me you won't ever become like your dad." Tears fell down her cheeks.

"I promise, Mother." What else was I supposed to say? Unfortunately, my word was a bond to me, so that made me stuck telling Mother everything.

"Thank you, dear," Mother said after I stopped talking. "Now eat." She let go of my hand and went to the oven for biscuits.

"Can I have the notebooks back?" I asked cautiously. I was scared Mother would go emotional and burn them if I pushed too hard.

"Of course," Mother said and handed me the notebooks. Way easier than I'd expected.

"That smells amazing," I told Mother as she poured gravy over my biscuits. Sometimes I almost forgot that she was a better cook then me. It was such a rare thing to see her in the kitchen. Her gift was taken for granted for so long.

"They are always amazing." Yup. Mother was definitely back to her normal, self-assured self. I stuffed a big bite of my biscuit in my mouth so I didn't have to reply.

After a few moments, Mother spoke up. "What are the plans for today?"

"Library," I tried saying with a full mouth.

"Please swallow, dear," Mother said, refilling my coffee. I didn't realize I had finished the first cup. I was a Christian, but I would worship the person who invented coffee and pay the consequences later.

"I need to skip Zumba and head to the library this morning," I finally said after I swallowed.

"What's going on at the library?" Mother asked as she bit into another piece of bacon.

"My history lesson, I hope," I told her as I dipped my bacon in my gravy.

"You are taking this very serious," Mother said in a teasing tone.

"I recommend you do the same or Ethel the disciplinarian will make you pay," I said with a smirk.

"You do have a point," Mother said, and we both laughed. I did not want to face the wrath of Ethel for failing to be prepared for class on Friday.

"What about you?" I asked, realizing I had no clue how Mother used to spend her days at the senior community.

"Florence and I are driving to Longview," Mother said as she sipped her coffee. She didn't elaborate on her statement.

"Fine, I'll ask. What are you two doing there?" I started this conversation, so I guessed it was my job to continue it.

"One of Florence's boys just moved there," Mother said. "He has tons of guns he got from his uncles and some of his other family members. His wife is pregnant and wants most of them gone, so we are picking them up."

"What are you going to tell him you guys are doing with the guns?" I asked, panic rising in my chest. It was a risky move to get even more family involved.

"We are donating them to a foundation that helps veterans get back on their feet," Mother said.

"What? Is he going to believe that?" I didn't believe it, so I didn't see how anyone else would, either.

"He doesn't question his mother," she said. "He called me to make sure I was coming with her. He is convinced Florence has a gambling problem, so he's giving her the guns so she can sell them instead of using her savings to gamble."

I stopped chewing and stared. "Wait, he told you all that?"

"You'd be surprised what people tell me," Mother answered.

"I am surprised already." Either Mother was a great interrogator or people were confusing her with a Catholic priest. "Does Florence have a gambling problem?" I had been really antisocial the last few months, so I was out of touch with the gossip in town.

"Of course not, but she is supporting the horrible habits of her younger son," Mother clarified. It made sense. I'd heard that the son was hooked on meth.

"That is not going to end well," I said, but I knew it was an understatement.

"Florence knows, but a mother would die for her kids," Mother said and stared deep in my eyes.

I broke the eye contact. There were way too many emotions going around this early in the morning. "In that case, be careful." I took the empty plate to the sink.

"You too, dear," Mother said. "It seems too many people are watching us now." That last statement sounded menacing.

"Of course, Mother," I wasn't sure what else to say. "I'm going to go get ready. I want to be the first one at the library. Maybe I won't be there all day, then. Please let Maria know I'll pay her when I get back." I headed out the door and towards my room.

Mother and the cats stayed in the kitchen, probably munching on bacon and drinking coffee. Doing my hair and makeup was going to take me at least forty-five minutes. If I hurried, I could get to the library by eight thirty. If I didn't hurry, I'd run into the Zumba crowd, then I'd never make it out.

I was very proud of myself when it only took me thirty-five minutes to get my hair and makeup done. It had been a lot faster than I'd expected, but I had the lady at Dillard's to thank. The technique she'd shown me was amazing and made things so much easier. She promised I'd get better with practice. Applying makeup was kind of like riding a bike. Slowly, it all came back and you remembered exactly what to do.

The celebration continued when I was able to get to the library by eight thirty when they opened. I even had time to grab one of those fancy coffees from the Seven Eleven in town on my way there.

Before entering the library, I finished my coffee in the car. I was pretty sure libraries still had strict rules regarding food and drinks inside. Ethel had given me a list of books that would be great as reference materials for my course. She wanted me to start with world history before covering US history. I was so rusty on my history that I needed as many reference materials as possible.

I had an active library card, but I hadn't been to it since my divorce. For a small town, we had a very impressive library. Minnie told me the library was where all the rich people in town donated money as their tax write-off. The practice seemed a bit odd, but I was grateful for the results. The library was two stories, so a lot of people from the nearby communities used it. They had three staff members on call at all times—not bad for a small town.

As soon as I finished my coffee, I made my way inside. I waved at the two librarians on duties, peering cautiously for the third but not finding her. She must be upstairs. I only recognized Monica, who was around my age and been at the library for at least two decades. Monica normally scared me because she always wore too much makeup and her hair was huge. She was also the biggest gossip in town. I made it a point to avoid her and anyone she was associated with.

Ethel's notes were amazing. Not only did she provide the name of the book, she also included the location in the library. I headed towards the non-fiction section and started my search. The library was quiet but soft sounds started filling the place as more people came in. The sounds were never loud, just the sounds people made when they moved around a place. Finding Ethel's book did not take me long, so I decided to make a quick trip towards the young adult fantasy section. It had been an accident the day I discovered YA fantasy, but ever since, I'd been hooked.

The shelves had several new books. I inspected all the covers and read the backs of several. I was in the middle of reading the back of a new series I found that took place in Texarkana when I heard my name being whispered. I stood very still, pretending not to hear anything. But the voices grew louder and purer, so I focused until the words became clearer.

"All this time we've thought of her as the victim, but the truth finally came out," Monica said. "My friend's mother talked to Todd's second cousin who said Todd admitted over drinks that he caught Angela messing around with Judge James. I knew he wasn't as innocent as everyone thought he was."

I couldn't breathe. My stomach turned. I needed to maintain my composure and not make a scene. Slowly I grabbed my books and with my head held high, I sauntered right to the front desk. I smiled at the other librarian, but I wasn't listening to a word he said. It took everything inside of me to walk out the door with my head still raised. I was convinced everyone was staring at me, but I was too filled with shame and horror to care. Somehow, not for the first time, I'd become the topic of the town gossip.

The air was cool and it felt good against my cheeks. Tears were threatening to rush out, so I ran to my car. I climbed inside and locked all the doors. This couldn't be happening to me, not again. But I needed to calm down. I couldn't face Mother this way. After several deep breaths, I decided to do something wild, something I had never done. I drove to the movie theater in Atlanta. According to the paper, the theater was playing a matinee special for seniors Tuesday, Wednesday, and Thursday. I wanted to hide and not think for a while, and the movies seemed like the safest option.

Chapter Nineteen

*B*y the time I pulled in my drive way, it was midday. The only car around was Ethel's. I debated turning around, but I didn't. Where else would I go? I couldn't keep running away, not when I lived here. The backdoor to the backyard was open, and for a moment I considered sneaking in and heading to the bunker. It would be futile, though. They'd see my car, and when I showed up later, I'd have to explain where I went and why.

Grow a pair, I repeated Ethel's words to myself. The thought was so scandalous it made my cheeks grow warm.

After a deep breath, maybe two, I steeled myself and headed inside.

"Hi Angela," Minnie said as soon as I arrived.

"How did you know it was me?" I asked as I looked around the room. Only Minnie and Hector were in the living room, working on something, but I could hear Ethel rustling around in the kitchen, probably with Julio.

"Easy. Bonnie and Clyde were going crazy when they heard your car," Minnie said with a smile as the guilty culprits strolled my way.

Clyde stood on his back legs, reaching for to me to pick him up. Bonnie just rubbed my legs over and over. I picked Clyde up, and the minute I did, he rubbed his head on my chin. I could always fool people, but never my cats. They could sense how upset I was. I rubbed Clyde's back softly and a tear rolled down my cheek.

"Angie dear, what's going on?" Minnie asked, getting up from the sofa.

"Nothing, I'm fine," I mumbled.

"What happened?" Ethel rushed in the room.

"Nothing," I replied.

"You are a terrible liar, child. Spill it," Ethel demanded with her arms crossed over her chest.

"Stop yelling at her, Ethel. You are making it worse," Minnie told her as she dragged me to the couch.

I didn't have the energy to fight it. I sat on the couch, holding Clyde as Bonnie jumped on my lap. Both cats were purring and refused to move. I was sure if anyone tried to touch me now, their claws would come out swinging.

"Here, Ms. Angela," Julio handed me a glass of water.

"Thank you dear," I reached for the glass, but Ethel took it.

"She needs something stronger." Ethel headed to the kitchen with the glass.

Everyone was silent, even Hector. I rubbed both of my cats and refused to look at anyone. Ethel came back with a cup of what looked like coffee and cream. Normally I liked my coffee black, but I didn't care. I took one sip and found out the cream wasn't cream at all. It was something a lot stronger.

"Oh Lord," I said to her, trying to push the mug back in her hand.

"Irish cream. Drink," Ethel said as she moved her hands away from me.

I took another sip. The liquor warmed me from the inside out. It didn't take long to go over what I'd heard, but it hurt deep.

"That bitch!" Ethel yelled.

"Ethel, language," I told her.

"You should start cursing every once in a while. It will make you feel so much better," Ethel told me.

"I agree," Minnie added with a chuckle.

I rolled my eyes. That was exactly what I needed, to start cursing like a sailor. Because that would help me so much.

"Why do you care what they say, Ms. Angela?" Hector asked after the ladies calmed down.

"People have been talking about me for so long. I had just hoped it had stopped," I answered him honestly.

"Hector is right, though. Why do you care?" Julio asked. "You are not friends with any of those people, so why does it matter what they say?"

"We live in a very small town, dear," Minnie jumped in. "Sometimes our reputation is all we have." She gave my hands a tight squeeze.

"Reputation doesn't pay the bills." Hector's voice held a

tinge of anger. "All those holier-than-the-Pope people are a bunch of hypocrites. When our dad left, where were all the good people to help Mother? And her reputation was good. Still, nobody showed up." Hatred hid behind the depths of Hector's eyes, and his words came out as a growl.

"Our mother listens to this minister from Houston all the time, and he says it's not what people call you that matters. It's how you respond." Julio took a seat next to his brother.

"That is wisdom," Ethel said in a softer voice. "We could all learn from it."

"I know," I mumbled. "But now they are talking about me and James. I never even talked to him before this campaign." I was getting choked up again. He was a good man and his reputation could be ruined just because he'd chosen to associate with me.

"Meow," Clyde replied.

"That's why he's doing it," Ethel said.

"Who?" Minnie asked.

"That two-timing idiot Todd. Who else?" Ethel paced up and down the living room.

"What?" I asked.

"He is trying to ruin James's campaign. He knows if you start spilling his dirty little secrets, he is doomed," Ethel said, waving her arms around.

"How does he even know I'm helping?" I asked her, feeling like a deer caught by bright headlights.

"Honey, we called over four-hundred people in this county last night," Ethel said, and I slapped my forehead, feeling like an idiot. "He took it personal."

"It is personal. He took everything from me." The words came out louder than I'd wanted. "Having him in charge of the law while we run guns is like tempting fate."

"That means he is scared," Hector said.

"Scared of me?" I had a hard time believing that.

"I agree," Minnie said. "The military calls this a preemptive strike." I forgot that back in her youth, Minnie had served in the medic Corp, so she had lots of military references.

"I can't stay on the campaign. It would ruin James," I told the group.

"Who said you were on the campaign?" Ethel said, and the look she gave me was positively wicked.

"What?" I asked, raising my eyebrows. Lately, it seemed I had no clue what the heck was happening. I'd never been confused so often in my life.

"Barbara is helping in the campaign. You were just an innocent bystander forced to help," Ethel explained. "Hence the horrible calling numbers."

"It was unpleasant to watch," Minnie added.

"Okay, what are you two talking about?" I finally asked.

"This is war and we will fight rumors with rumors," Ethel said. "And we have years of practice. Hector, Julio, tell Maria we are going to need her help."

"Do I want to know what you are thinking?" I asked Ethel.

"Don't worry dear, we got this," Minnie said. "I'll get in touch with your mother and fill her in. We need Ms. Barbara to get to work. Todd has declared war, and this time he has gone too far." She got up from the couch and headed towards the kitchen.

"What am I supposed to do?" I asked Ethel, who'd gone back to pacing.

"You need to tell that cute little judge that you can't help him anymore, but that the rest of us are in," Ethel explained.

"Today?" I was not ready to see James again.

"Yes dear, before the rumor mill catches him blind," Ethel told me. "But before that, you need to freshen up, eat something, and maybe take a nap."

"All those things sound like great ideas," Hector agreed.

"Don't even think about it, young man. We still have school work," Ethel gave poor Hector a look that froze him in his tracks.

"Yes ma'am," he replied as he lowered his head. "We could help!" he shouted less than ten seconds later. "We could slash all his tires." A huge smile of anticipation shone from him after he'd made his announcement.

"Not yet, my dear Che Guevara," Ethel said, but this time she was smiling. "We will need those guerrilla tactics later." She turned her attention to me. "In the meantime, you need to get a grip on yourself. You are no longer a dependent housewife. You are a furious arms dealer who is going to take the competition out of the equation. Got it?" She gave me a hard stare, and for a minute, I wondered if she could see straight inside me.

"Got it," I didn't feel like any of those things, but I had my faith and I knew it would give me the courage I needed to find my inner strength and become who I needed to be.

I wiped my face and slowly lowered the cats to the couch. It was a struggle to get up but having six pairs of eyes watching gave me a new kind of motivation.

"A nap and a shower sound great," I told the group as I headed towards my room. Bonnie and Clyde were right behind me.

"Finish the coffee first, and then rest," Ethel called after me.

"Will do," I replied and closed the door behind me.

Don't cry, don't cry, I repeated to myself. I was not going to shed another tear. I was not helpless. It didn't matter what people said, except it was a lot easier to think than to believe.

I shook myself, knowing I needed to focus on the problems at hand. Something would come up. It had to. I decided against a shower and made myself a bath. A long soaking would do me wonders.

Chapter Twenty

I had driven all the way to Linden to find James. The drive
was heart wrenching. What was I supposed to tell him?
Would he even care if I quit his campaign team? Honestly, he would
probably be glad I was gone. If it wasn't for me, he wouldn't be in
the middle of this messy scandal. James had the cleanest reputation
out of anyone, and not just in Lynden, but in the whole county. One
day being around me and now he was considered a home wrecker.
Were men able to be considered home wreckers or was that a term
designated only to women?

Smack dab in the middle of a crisis and still I found myself
questioning random stuff. I needed to focus and leave the
philosophical questions for another day. Unfortunately, I couldn't
break out of my own head. Plus, I couldn't find anything to do but
think. The radio stations had nothing interesting happening at this
time of day. A little while ago, the boys recommended I get satellite
radio, and at the time, I'd thought it sounded like a crazy splurge. I
never went anywhere, so why would I ever spend that kind of cash?
Now, I kind of wished I'd indulged a little.

The clock in my car read four thirty by the time I pulled up to
the one-story house James was using as his campaign headquarters.
It had a quaint Victorian feel that stuck out like a sore thumb against
the rest of the town. The house was located on a beautiful lot on
Main Street, away from the main city and near the cemetery. I didn't
know how I would feel living that close to all those dead people.
Yes, I was perfectly aware all those people were buried, but I had
watched enough scary movies to question if they would stay that
way.

I pulled into the driveway and parked behind a very pristine
looking red Ford Focus. James did not look like the kind of guy to
drive a Focus. As I turned the engine off, Jenny rushed from the

house carrying some large boxes, which she shoved into the trunk of the car in less than five seconds. Now, I could see *her* driving that car. It was a perfect match.

"That is a lot of trunk space," I told Jenny as I strolled up beside her. I'd never been much into cars, but I'd dismissed the Focus as a potential vehicle for me. After seeing all the trunk space, I might have to reconsider. A lot of guns could fit inside there.

"Main reason I bought it," Jenny told me. "Best purchase ever. I have totally made my money back with it." She slammed the trunk and turned to give me her undivided attention.

I wondered how she was able to make her money back but decided against asking. Last thing I needed was to be an accessory to some strange crime. Unless Jenny was smuggling people in that trunk, I wasn't sure how she would earn her money back.

"To what do we owe the pleasure of this visit, Ms. Angela?" Jenny asked, leaning against her car. "You are a bit far from Sunshine." Her eyes went from the top of my head to the tips of my shoes. It made me a bit uncomfortable.

"I was hoping to speak with you and James," I told her, even though I actually just wanted to speak with James, but I thought admitting that out loud would sound rude.

"You do know we have phones here," Jenny told me as she pulled her cell from her pocket and waved it at me.

"True." My palms were starting to get sweaty as I realized I was sounding more and more insane by the minute. "However, I feel like I might be letting you guys down, and I prefer to do that kind of thing in person." It was a total lie. I would've rather called, sent a text, anything other than coming in person, but Minnie and Florence hadn't given me that option.

"I don't like the sound of that," Jenny said, pushing away from her car.

"I won't be able to help with the campaign anymore," I told Jenny, keeping my gaze focused on her. If this situation turned into a staring contest, Jenny would be the winner. She had the most piercing stare I'd ever experienced. It was so intense that I had to look away first.

"Please don't tell me you have been listening to the rumor mill," Jenny said as she inched a bit closer.

"Wow," I said out loud, then I added, "You heard already?" I knew the Sunshine rumor mill was good, but I hadn't known they were *that* good.

"We've been getting calls all day, so trust me, we know," Jenny said. She shook her head, but the sharp edges of her haircut hardly moved.

"Doesn't it bother you?" I asked Jenny.

"Rumors are part of the job. I won't lose my mind over it," she told me right before she headed towards the house.

"You definitely don't know the power of rumors in a small town," I told her.

"Overrated, Angela," Jenny told me as she left. "People will believe whatever they want to. Rumors just give them the excuse they need to justify their beliefs."

Listening to Jenny made me realize she had never lived in a small town. I had no idea where she came from, but she was speaking like a true city girl.

I was searching for a response when James pulled up in an old-school Toyota truck. Funny enough, the old truck only made him look more elegant to me.

"Good afternoon, Angela," James said as he climbed out of his truck. When he turned to face me, the smile beaming from him made my toes curl with excitement.

"Hi James," I said, trying to avoid making eye contact while not coming off ill-mannered at the same time. Those two things did not go together at all.

"What are you doing here?" James asked, erasing the distance between us in no time.

"She is quitting the campaign because of the rumor mill," Jenny shouted from the doorway before heading inside.

"What? Why?" James asked, getting way too comfortable in my space.

What was the deal with this group of people? Did they have a complete disregard for personal space?

"It would not be good for your campaign to be associated with me," I told him as I stared at my new pair of Mary Jane flats like they'd turned into the most interesting things in the world.

"I think I should be the judge of that," James said, tilting my chin up with the tips of his fingers.

"You don't know Todd like I do," I tried to explain. "He is a cunning, manipulative snake in the grass. He will use anything to tarnish your reputation so he can win."

"Angela, please trust me," James said in a softer voice. "This is not my first rodeo."

I don't trust many people, especially men," I blurted before I could think about my words. As soon as I saw the look of sadness cross his features, I wanted to take it back, but I couldn't. Not when it was the absolute truth. Todd had destroyed my faith in the male species, making it impossible for me to trust them.

"That sounds like a really lonely life," James said, then he backed away from me.

"I'll make it," I said, biting the inside of my cheek. "I'm sorry for taking up your time. Mother and her friends will continue to help." I turned, not able to face him. "I'm sorry again."

"Do you honestly think the rumors will stop that easily?" James asked.

His words made me stop and face him. "I know they won't," I admitted. "But I also know Mother and her friends are getting ready to launch their own campaign. This is about to get ugly, so I need to stay away." I shrugged, then made to walk away again.

"Wait." James grabbed my hand. My pulse jolted to high speed while my hand tingled under his touch. I focused on my breathing, trying to make it come normally, but I had a feeling I was fighting a losing battle. My eyes moved to the hand he still held, and he released it.

"I'm sorry Angela." James shoved his hands in his pockets. "Would you at least have dinner with me? I still want to thank you for all your help."

"I have a feeling that would make the rumor mill worse," I forced the words out, but inside I really wanted to say yes.

"Maybe it will, but I really don't care," James told me. "You are such an amazing person."

"You give me too much credit. I'm not as good as you think I am," I replied. "Cass County can't afford to be without a judge or to have Todd as their new one. Good bye, James."

Before he could say anything else, I dashed back to my car. James had a strange effect on me, and I knew I'd never be able hold my ground if I didn't leave now. Much to my dismay, he didn't try to stop me again, so I climbed in my car and took off back to Sunshine.

If the drive to Lynden was painful, the drive back home was murderous. A sadness overtook me, so much that I had to fight off tears. I had no idea when it had happened, but I wanted to date James, and I had to get that crazy idea out of my head before I actually allowed it to happen.

Instead, I needed a plan to get rid of the thugs I had dealings with, and then I needed a plan to get rid of Todd. As I concentrated on driving, I hoped a brilliant idea would pop into my mind.

It was going to be a *long* drive home.

Chapter Twenty-One

Mother's early schedule didn't last long, and I wasn't complaining. This Thursday morning, I had the kitchen all to myself since she was in bed. Mother had left me a note on the counter that the boys were coming over to do school work at eight. I wasn't used to having people over on a regular basis, especially in the morning. That didn't leave me a lot of time to do my morning routing. I rushed to feed the kitties, make a batch of chocolate chip muffins, and brew two pots of coffee. There wasn't enough time to indulge in my favorite pastime of doing the daily crossword puzzle. Without wasting any time, I headed to shower.

There was something magical about showers. I couldn't explain it, but for some reason great ideas always hit me when I shampooed my hair. Okay, sometimes the ideas weren't great but more like crazy. Today was one of the latter. I was immobile, covered in bubbles, when this insane idea hit me.

That is impossible. I could never pull that off, I told myself as the water washed away my shampoo. The shower smelled of rose petals, so I closed my eyes to breathe it all in. *But what if I could find a way? Would I do it?* Could I purposely go out of my way to hurt someone? I didn't want to, but I was tired of being everyone's punching bag.

I was still battling my indecision when I strolled in the living room. Julio, Hector, and Mother were there, which I'd expected, but Minnie had arrived too. They were talking in hushed voices, at least until I walked in when they just stopped talking altogether.

"What is going on?" I asked the group.

"Good morning to you too," Mother said, crossing her arms like she was Queen Elizabeth.

"My apologies to everyone. Good morning," I said, giving them a small curtsy. "Now what's going on?" I moved a little closer to them.

"Nothing dear, just the normal stuff," Minnie replied, but her eyes were red.

"Minnie, what happened?" If anyone had hurt her, I would strangle them with my bare hands.

"Honey, I'm good," Minnie replied with a weak smile I knew she tried to force but had failed miserably.

"Mother?" I asked hoping she would tell me.

Instead she got up and headed to the kitchen. "More coffee everyone?"

"Hector?" I looked at him first since he was closer.

"Your mom would kill me," Hector whispered as he peered over my shoulder to watch Mother.

"Chicken," I muttered as I glanced towards the kitchen as well. I didn't mean it. In fact, I wasn't brave around Mother either.

"Julio, please," I begged, holding my hands together in supplication. Maybe Julio would feel sorry for me and speak.

"Oh," Julio whined, but then he angled his head to the side, and I knew I had him. "The Silver Hair Gang are getting kicked out of the senior home for helping in the campaign."

"What?" I'd wanted to scream but instead the question came out as a squeak. "They can't do that."

"Oh, they can dear," Mother said as she handed me a cup of coffee. "It appears our dear Todd has friends in the Board of Directors. They convinced the board that the ladies were trouble makers instigating demise on the premise."

"He doesn't appreciate when the tables are turned and rumors are about him," Minnie said, letting out a forced laugh. "Relax, Angela. We are going to be okay." Her calmness only made my fury stronger.

"Of course you are going to be okay. You are all moving in here," I announced. "Call Florence and Ethel, we are picking them up today. Hector, Julio, do you guys think your uncle would help us again?"

"Absolutely," Hector said with a smile. He jumped up from the sofa, gave Minnie a hug, and headed out the door.

"Your mother is my hero," I told Julio.

"Angela, you don't have to do this," Minnie told me as she wiped tears from her eyes.

"You three are my family," I told Minnie. "You will never be neglected or alone as long as I'm here. You will always have a home here. This is also my fault, so I will fix it." My feet moved of their own accord and before I knew it, I paced the length of the room.

"Angela, you did not make Todd be an asshole," Mother told me. I was so mad that I didn't even correct her for swearing.

"You are right about that, but I should have taken the offense a long time ago," I said.

"I have to agree with that," Minnie said. "You should have put that punk in his place a long time ago."

If I was honest with myself, I could never hurt someone to save myself. That was not the case when it came to those I loved, though. How could any normal person get three old ladies kicked out of an assisted living center? What kind of human being would stoop that low? Even for Toddy, this was pathetic.

"We need to stop him, no matter the cost," I told the group.

"Sign me up," Mother said in a rush.

"I just need a computer guru to help us," I told them.

"I don't know about a guru, but I can find you a hacker," Julio announced.

"How do you know a hacker?" I asked him. I looked at Mother and Minnie for support, but their eyes were on Julio.

"It's not that impressive, trust me," Julio told us. "He's my cousin."

"Do you think he would be interested in helping us after school?" I asked Julio, praying our luck was finally turning around.

"He is not in school. Andres got kicked out," Julio said without any emotion.

"Do we want to know why he got kicked out?" Mother asked as she gave Julio a careful look.

"Because he graduated himself from high school." Julio clarified, but it didn't really make anything clearer.

"Am I missing something?" Minnie asked in a confused voice. "I thought that was the purpose of high school."

"Yes, if you went to class and did the required work," Julio said with a smirk.

"Julio, what did he actually do?" I asked.

"He hacked into the school system and graduated himself from school," Julio told us. "Nobody would have noticed, except Andres is only thirteen."

Okay, I might be a little impressed.

"We need him," I told Julio.

"Sounds like we have a new student," Mother told me.

"Could you do us the honor of asking your cousin to join us?" I asked.

"I doubt he would want to enroll in school again, but he happens to be at the house right now," Julio told me with a wicked smile.

"Why is he at your house?" Mother asked, crossing her arms over her chest.

"My aunt is afraid to leave him unsupervised." Julio shook his head. "Four days out of the week while my aunt is at work, Andres hangs out with Mother," he explained.

"Perfect, joining the school would be great for his social life," I told Julio. "Check with your mother first, but we need Andres here."

Without any delays, Julio bounced off the couch and disappeared out the backdoor.

"In the meantime, you two need to call the ladies and tell them our plan," I ordered. "We are moving you guys out of that hell hole today." I couldn't let Todd have this much control over the people I loved.

"Angela has a point," Mother concurred. "We need to get you guys out of there before Ethel strangles someone."

"Agreed. We don't have murder money," I told Minnie. "We might have enough cash to cover a couple of slaps, but not strangling."

Minnie's laughter filled the room, and I was happy to see the rose sheen back in her cheeks.

"Are you going to be okay?" Mother asked.

"I'm sure I can handle a thirteen-year-old, even if he is a hacker," I said.

"In that case, we are taking off. We have lots of packing to do," Mother got up and grabbed her purse from the coffee table.

"I love you, Angela," Minnie said as she gave me a soft kiss on my forehead.

"I love you, too," I told her, giving her arm a gentle squeeze. "We will meet you as soon as we settle things here."

Mother turned and walked out the door, and Minnie followed after a nod of her head. Then, Bonnie and Clyde strolled out of the bedroom, hopped on the coffee table, and stared at me as if they already knew what was happening.

"Sorry sweeties, we are getting more roommates," I told my cats and rubbed both of their heads.

"Meow," replied Bonnie. Clyde just purred. I feared my cats were getting too used to strangers in the house.

The back door opened, and Julio and Hector dragged a small boy behind them. I assumed the new kid was Andres. He was less than five feet tall, very thin, and wore glasses. His dark hair curled at the ends, making him look even younger.

Julio shoved Andres in front of him. The brothers stood guard on both side of Andres. For a moment, I wondered if he was planning to run.

"You are the Cat Lady?" Andres asked, giving me an unimpressed look.

"You must be the hacker," I retorted, but he only held my gaze. It told me he definitely wasn't intimidated by adults.

"Are you planning to give me a lecture on life choices?" Andres was smart and quick on his feet. I liked him.

"Sorry, no. I'm not your mother," I told the little brat, and that shut him right up. "I'm planning to offer you a job."

The kid had been bouncing on the balls of feet, but he stopped suddenly. "A job?"

"According to Julio, you are good with computers," I said. "I need a few credit cards made, some guns ordered from Russia, and a very nasty man framed for it. Can you do it?" I was going big or going home, as the boys kept saying.

"Are you serious?" Andres's eyes got huge and he licked his lips.

"Like a heart attack," I said with a grin. "Can you do it?"

"Are your cats covered in fur?" he replied.

"Meow," Clyde answered.

"See, even that one agrees," Andres said, picking at his shirt like it was covered in lint. "What's the catch? If I agree to do it, do I have to join this stupid alternative school you created?"

"If you can pull this off, and we don't go to jail, you will be compensated for your efforts," I told my little hustler. "If you enjoy working with us, I'll pay you to come to school here." I held his stare as he considered my words.

"You will pay me to go to school?" Andres glanced at Julio, who only smiled like a proud parent.

"Consider going to school a condition of employment," I told Andres. "It is only fair to pay you for your troubles." I leaned back on the couch as I spoke.

"If I accept it, when do I start?" Andres asked.

"Now," I told him. "It's Thursday morning and we need this delivery here for Monday morning. Can you make that happen?" Time was of the essence, so I hoped Andres was as good as his cousin told me he was.

"I'm in," Andres announced and Julio and Hector both gave him fist bumps. "But I'm going to need a computer. As part of my probation, I'm not allowed to own one." His eyes searched the room.

"You are in luck; I just purchased one recently," I told him, heading to my bedroom to get the computer. I had never turned it on, but it had a tower and a large monitor. I hoped that was all he needed.

When I returned, I handed Andres the tower and monitor. He set everything on the coffee table, and in less than five minutes, he had everything set up.

"Please tell me you have Internet?" Andres asked.

"I do," I answered, even though I'd never used it.

"Good," Andres told me, clicking some stuff on the laptop I couldn't see. "I will need to install a few precautions before we get started, as well as masking your new IP."

I had no idea what Andres was talking about, so I just nodded. "Pull this off and you get an automatic A in computer class," I said.

"I like how you roll, Cat Lady," Andres told me.

"Call me Angela. Better yet, make it Ms. Angela. That way you don't get in trouble with your aunt," I corrected him.

"Ms. Angela, you have a deal," Andres walked over and we shook hands. I had never done a criminal deal with a thirteen-year-old.

"Let's see what you can do," I told Andres. "I need to help the Silver Hair Gang get moved. Andres, you are in charge of the house with Bonnie and Clyde while I'm gone. Can you handle that?"

"You just met me and you are leaving me in charge of your place?" Andres's wide eyes moved to Julio.

"You are family, dear," I called from the door to my room. "If you steal from me, you are stealing from yourself. I know you won't do that. But if you think you need it, I'll get you a babysitter."

I smirked. "Do you need one?"

"Of course not," Andres said, but he didn't look up from the computer.

"If you want, Julio and Hector could keep you company and watch the house while you work." I had to remind myself he was still thirteen, regardless of the little attitude he carried with him.

"Don't you need us at the home?" Hector asked from behind.

"We do need your packing skills," I told Hector and Julio

"In that case, we are going," Hector replied.

"In that case, give Andres a tour of the house and show him what is in the fridge in case he gets hungry," I told the boys, then I headed inside my bedroom.

I grabbed a piece of paper from my night stand and wrote down my social security number, names, addresses, phone numbers, and other important information Andres might need. By the time I got back to the living room, Andres had made himself comfortable on the couch. I marched over and handed him the piece of paper, which he took with a smile.

"Remind me not to make you mad," Andres said.

"Then make sure to do your homework, otherwise I'll be furious." I raised my eyebrows and gave him a hard look.

He averted his gaze back to the computer after he nodded.

"Hector, Julio, ready?" I asked the boys as they came in the living room by way of the kitchen.

"We are, and Uncle will meet meeting us there," Hector said.

"Great, let's go then," I told them. "Andres, I left you my number on that paper. If you need anything, give me a call. We will be back as soon as we can."

"I'll be here," Andres replied, not bothering to look up.

I prayed silently that I was doing the right thing, then the boys and I headed out the door to meet the rest of the team. Todd had crossed the line when he went after them, and for them I was willing to do anything.

Even what I was about to do.

Chapter Twenty-Two

When leaving a retirement community, the amount of paperwork required was unreasonable. It wasn't that way when getting kicked out. In fact, there was almost no paperwork. By the time the boys and I made it to the community, the forms were filled out, notices were signed, and even the ladies' rooms had been packed. Florence was devastated. The people packing their stuff were ruthless and just threw everything in boxes. Minnie was trying to console her, but Florence couldn't stop crying. I was sure those were tears of anger, but they still broke my heart.

Mother had her hands full holding Ethel back from murdering the staff. Hector had been in constant communication with his uncle, and he was coming in ten minutes behind us. Our plan was simple, get the Silver Hair Gang out of this hell hole as quickly as possible. They didn't need to be humiliated any more.

"Did they hurt you?" Julio was the first one to reach the ladies as they stood in front of their former apartments.

"It was an accident," Florence said as she rubbed the side of her arm.

"Let me see," I said as I reached her.

Florence had a huge bruise at the top of her bicep. She also had hand prints on her wrists.

"What in the hell did they do to you?" Hector screamed.

"Nothing," Florence said between tears.

"They sent three men to clear our room and dragged us out," Ethel said, lifting her wrist to show her matching marks.

"Those bastards." Julio's features scrunched as he looked around the room for the culprits. I knew I should scold him for swearing, but I was too mad to care.

"Julio, take photos of all their bruises," I told him.

"Why?" Julio asked, even while he got his camera out.

"The one thing I learned from my cheating ex is that you always need evidence," I said, grabbing Florence's hand gently. "This is not over, and we need to document all the suffering and pain they caused. Make sure to get really good angles."

"Got it," Julio said, crouching down to photograph Florence's biceps like a professional.

"I'll get photos of the rooms," Hector volunteered.

I nodded. These fools did not know who they were messing with.

"Mother, let's take the ladies back to the house," I said. "The boys' uncle will be coming over to pick up the rest of their stuff. We can take what's necessary and have him put the rest in storage."

"We still have plenty of room in our storage unit," Mother said. "We can meet them there and show them the unit."

"That would be great," I said. "I need to make a little side trip and might need Ethel's or Florence's help," the last part I whispered to mother.

"We'll talk in the car," Mother said, barely moving her lips.

"Ms. Angela, they are here," Hector said as he ran out of the room. "Going to meet them at the front. Our uncle said he brought extra help and even a couple of dollies. We should be done and out of here in no time." He disappeared, and Julio followed without asking.

"Okay ladies, point at the boxes you are going to need for the next couple of days," I told the ladies. "Those are coming with us now and the rest will go to storage until we sort it all out." I knew this was going to crush them, but we needed to get them out of here as fast as possible.

The gossip mill had started. The other residents gave us strange glances. I had no idea if Mother or Ethel was more volatile in that moment. If either of them got their hands on any of the staff, even the gossiping neighbors, blood would drench the floors.

Hector and Julio were back in under two minutes with a group of men ready to work. I was so grateful for them. The boys explained the situation to the men, and they wasted no time as they ran into the rooms and came back out carrying boxes.

"Gracias, Mr. Carlos," I told the uncle.

"Siempre, Miss Angela," he replied in half Spanish and half English, holding both of my hands and smiling.

"What does that mean?" Mother asked.

"Always," Julio added from behind me. "Mom has told him everything you have done for us. He has been meaning to say thank you to you sooner, so this works."

It was Minnie's turn to wipe the tears from her cheeks. This was a very emotional day. I couldn't take it anymore. The ladies were getting kicked out like wild dogs. Nobody deserved this.

"Okay ladies, we got work to do," I told them right before I pulled Florence and Minnie with me. "We need to get out of here."

"Angela is right, let's go," Mother told her best friends. I wasn't sure how she did it, but she got them to move. Together, we walked out the front doors of the retirement home.

"Keep your heads up, ladies," Mother told the Silver Hair Gang and all three of their backs straightened as they snapped their heads up, marching out like they were the leaders of a parade. Mother even stopped and turned to wave at all the bystanders. So scandalous!

I couldn't help it when I laughed. I had to with that exit scene. It was priceless. They would not have the last word. Mother made it a point to make sure everyone knew they were not defeated. This was not a punishment, only a temporary reassignment. By the time we made it to the far end of the parking lot, my cheeks hurt from all my fake smiles.

"The boys did well," Ethel said, the first one to speak.

"What do you mean?" I asked her as I massaged my cheeks.

"They got a large truck just for us." She pointed to the cargo truck parked in front of the center.

"I'm pretty sure that was all Ana. She thinks of everything," I replied.

"We need to get her a gift," Florence said from behind her sister.

"I agree," Minnie added, and her voice was hoarse.

"Okay Angela, what do you need help with?" Mother asked me in a soft tone. The rest of the Silver Hair Gang surrounded us.

"I think I have a plan to pay back our favorite two-timing cheater *and* get rid of our blackmailers," I whispered so nobody else would hear us.

"I'm in," Ethel said.

"Me too," Minnie and Florence said in unison.

"You guys don't even know the plan," I told them, shaking my head.

"You have a plan and that is all that matters," Ethel said.

"This could end really badly for us," I added.

"We will die trying," Minnie told me. "What do you need?"

"We need a U-Haul rented under Todd's name for Monday," I told the ladies. "Could we get your nephew to help us?" I asked.

They had two nephews from their deceased brother. Those boys adored their aunts, but I was afraid to put them in a bad position.

"Consider it done," Florence said as she pulled her cell from her bra. Why did older ladies use their bra as their personalized carrying bags? That was so weird.

While I pondered the impracticality of sticking cash, phones, keys, and all other sorts of random stuff into a bra, Hector and Julio came running back.

"Ms. Angela, our uncle said to go ahead to the storage facility," Julio said a little out of breath. "They will only be fifteen minutes behind, but he figured the ladies would like to get as far away from here as possible."

"That sounds great," I told Julio. "Are you guys coming with us, or your uncle?"

"We are going to finish helping here, just in case one of those workers gets mouthy in English," Hector told me.

I didn't blame him. I wouldn't like having crazy people talking bad about me when I couldn't understand them.

"Be careful boys. These people are out for blood," Ethel told the boys, holding each one by a shoulder.

"We will," Hector told her. "We are getting out of there as fast as possible."

"Done, dear," Florence announced as she joined the group. "Hope you don't mind, but I took a few liberties. Considering that little Todd will be needing the truck very early Monday morning and he has offered extra for it to be delivered Sunday evening."

"That is perfect, Florence," I told her, giving her a high five.

"I watch a lot of crime movies," Florence explained. "It was only fair all the useless knowledge came in handy."

"I'm impressed," Mother said. "You do watch a lot of TV."

"As the kids say these days, don't judge," Florence told Mother as she waved her hand in the air. It was really funny watching such a modern move being done by such a classic lady.

"Thank you, Florence," I told her. "Let's get out of here

before someone starts listening to our conversation.

Each lady got in their respective car, so I jumped in mine and we drove off. We looked like a funeral procession, minus the speed limit. I was the second vehicle behind Minnie, and she was driving like she was trying out for NASCAR. Sure, I could have done the speed limit and been the slow one, but nobody wants to be outdone by the eighty-year-old grandma. With Minnie leading, the five of us flew across town like we'd just robbed a bank. It was exuberant and irresponsible all at once.

I was so happy the boys had stayed behind.

Chapter Twenty-Three

$\mathcal{B}$y the time we arrived back at my house it was almost three in the afternoon. Everyone in our group was starving. We had missed lunch with all the excitement. It took us longer than we expected to check each box to find the gang's necessary supplies. We needed to make sure the ladies had all their medicines, clothes, and personal artifacts, that way they would feel comfortable at my place.

The process was traumatizing for everyone. The crew at the facility didn't bother labeling anything. We found items mixed with all sorts of stuff and even some family heirlooms broken in the bottom of the box. My heart hurt just watching Minnie going through her stuff. Even Ethel, our usual rock, was in tears by the time we were done. I promised I would come back with them next week to get another unit and organize everything. Todd would pay for all the suffering he'd caused.

I had forgotten all about Andres until we made it in the house. It was a surprise to find him in the same place we'd left him. Bonnie and Clyde were perched over him on top of the sofa. If I wasn't emotionally drained, I would have laughed. It looked like Bonnie and Clyde were supervising poor Andres while he worked. The cats, as well as the young boy, were focused on the computer, barely blinking. Andres hadn't even noticed we'd come in. Neither had the cats for that matter. It stopped me in my tracks right in the foyer, so when the others walked in behind me, they stopped just the same, staring at the boy and the cats just like I was.

"Andres, are you okay?" Julio moved slowly towards his cousin.

Andres's head snapped up and he smiled brightly when he saw us. What had he been doing that he hadn't even registered our arrival?

"We did it!" Andres shouted, raising both hands straight in the air.

"Did what? And who is we?" Hector asked, inching forward as if he was approaching a wild animal.

"We finally found your Russian merchant," Andres said in an excited voice.

"Really?" I asked as I jogged forward, holding myself back as I almost tackled Andres.

Mother took the ladies to their new rooms. We were going to convert the small office/study room into a bedroom. That would give us four bedrooms in the house. Minnie agreed to take that one and the sisters would take the bedroom.

"It took us a while," Andres said, pointing at the screen as I sat next to him. "It was like chasing rabbits. We were all over the place. Even with the universal translator I installed, communication was tough. Does your cat speak Russian?" Andres asked, gesturing towards Clyde.

I was focused on the computer until Andres asked his last question. My head snapped up to stare at him. It was such a fast and sharp movement it caused my neck to pop.

"I don't even know if he understands English most of the time, so no way does he know Russian. Why do you ask?" I asked.

Andres was busy petting Clyde, who'd climbed down to sit next to him. "This one wouldn't leave me alone." His hands moved to Clyde's ear, inciting a loud purr.

"His name is Clyde and the one above your head is Bonnie," I told Andres.

"Those are awesome names for cats," Andres told me with the excitement that only kids had when they learned something new. I decided not to blow his mind by telling him the inspiration behind the famous names.

"Why do you think Clyde speaks Russian again?" I asked Andres as I tried to hide my smile.

"Meow," Clyde jumped in. I wasn't sure if he was agreeing or disagreeing with me.

"He was the one who found the right merchant," Andres said. "I was able to trace the name you left me to a Facebook group. By the way, I had to create a profile for you online after I encoded the IP address."

"I have no idea what that means. Do I need to remember all

that?" I asked him.

"Not at all," Andres told me. "Basically, I secured all the communications systems in the house. I need to give everyone a new WI-FI password."

"That sounds impressive and complicated," I told him.

"He has plenty of practice," Hector said as he leaned against the back of the couch with Bonnie. Julio was next to his brother, both of them looking at the computer.

"Don't be jealous just because you can't do it," Andres told his cousin, sticking out his tongue.

"I don't need to do it. That's why I got you," Hector replied, ruffling his cousin's hair.

"That is true. I'm good," Andres, said, wiping imaginary dirt from his shoulder. I had seen people do that in YouTube videos, but I had no idea what it meant.

"Thank God you are so modest. We would hate for your talents to go to your head," Julio told his cousin.

I had to agree with Julio. If Andres got any more arrogant, we'd probably have to hurt him.

"I'm not listening," Andres said, plugging his fingers in his ears.

"Can we get back to this thing?" I asked the three boys, nudging my head towards the screen.

"After an hour, I think he finally got tired of watching me struggle and decided to help me by pointing at the right one on the screen." Andres unplugged his ears and bounced with excitement while trying to pet Clyde. It looked so strange.

"This is great, but did you get them?" I had a long day so far and wanted to get to the point as quickly as possible.

"Fine," Andres said, this time sticking out his tongue at me.

"Andres, watch yourself," I told him, but I chuckled so I didn't sound very serious.

"You're no fun, Ms. Angela," Andres said.

"What?" I asked Andres "I just left you alone with my two favorite assistants to make your magic when you aren't even allowed to. How am I no fun?"

"Good point, nobody has ever given me that much freedom," Andres said, tapping his index finger against his cheeks. When he did that, I almost forgot he was a hacker. "The good news is we found one of the Russian distributors that handles our area. He will have a shipment for us on Sunday."

"From Russia?" It almost seemed impossible.

"Of course not. There is no way for a ship to get here that quickly," Andres corrected me. "Shipment is coming from Miami."

"That makes much more sense," I said, and Julio started laughing.

"We need to set up a drop point for them for this Sunday," Andres said.

"Well, sounds like we have work to do," I told the boys. "Let's start by making some food and we can go from there."

I went to the kitchen and left Julio talking computer stuff with Andres. I was in over my head and things were progressively getting worse. The house was big for one person, but it was going to be suffocating with five grown women. The Silver Hair Gang were a wreck and in less than four days I was supposed to deliver guns to a lunatic.

I lost it. Laughter erupted out of me, and it didn't stop. I had tears sliding out of my eyes and could hardly breathe by the time I finally came back to myself.

"Are you okay Ms. Angela?" Julio asked from the couch.

"Yes, I'm fine," I told him, but I didn't know if I was going into shock or suffering from hysteria. Maybe it was a little of both. "Debating between lasagna or chicken and dumplings."

"Lasagna," Andres yelled back.

"Well that settles it. Lasagna it is," I told the boys and went to the fridge to grab some ground beef.

Last week I was alone, broke, falling apart, and feeling like a failure in every aspect of my life. Now I had a house full of people, crazy problems, and actual money. Everyone looked to me to fix everything. I could run away, but what would that solve? I could go back to my original plan and off myself, but again, what would that do for anyone? Todd would've still gotten away with everything he'd done. The Silver Hair Gang would still be on the street, and the boys would still be working dead-end jobs to help support their family.

Dad, I need you, I said to myself as I pushed the ground beef around in the pan. Except, I might've been stabbing it as hard as I could. Probably not the best idea for the pan's health…

"If you keep breaking that up, you'll only have powder left," Mother told me as she stared at the pot.

I looked down and realized I had crumbled the poor meat. Mother took the spoon away from me and started mixing it. The seasoning rack was next to the stove, so Mother worked her magic.

"What's on your mind, Angela?" Mother asked in a soft voice so only I would hear.

"What am I doing?" I asked her. "I'm totally lost and in over my head."

"Angela relax, you are doing great," Mother told me.

"Mother, I'm not qualified to lead this group," I told her, feeling like an imposter.

Mother left her spoon in the pan and grabbed me. She held me by the shoulders and stared deep into my eyes. "Do you know what I see when I look at you?" Compassion filled her tone while tears brimmed in her eyes.

"No," I answered, then I held my breath because I was afraid of what she would say.

"I see your daddy," Mother told me, and the tears trickled down her cheeks. "I see a fierce and determined woman who would do anything for her loved ones. I see a woman who is creative, resourceful, and fearless. Just like your dad." Her arms came around me, and I held her, my whole body shaking as I held back the emotions threatening to explode from me.

"What is the worst thing that could happen?" Mother asked as she pulled away.

"We all go to jail, or maybe die," I told her with a chuckle.

"Jails are overpopulated. Trust me, nobody is giving a bunch of women the death sentence for a few guns," Mother said, wiping the tears from my face. "And death, we are all going to die someday. You know the saying 'everyone wants to go to heaven, but nobody wants to die?' Let go of that fear. Just ask yourself, what would your daddy do?"

"Call Bob and go have a beer," I said with a laugh, remembering what Dad did every time he got mad. With that, my shaking evaporated, so I looked at Mother with a steady gaze. "Mother, he called Bob," I repeated and slapped my head with my hand.

"He did say to call him for anything, didn't he?" Mother smiled and hugged me tighter this time. "Go, call. I'll finish dinner." She basically shoved me out of the kitchen. I glanced back only to find her grabbing another pot.

"Is everything okay?" Julio asked as I rushed through the living room towards my room.

"Yes, I just need to call Mr. Bob," I got out right before I went into my room. Clyde and Bonnie followed behind me, and as soon as we were all inside, I closed the door, pulled my cell phone out, and called Bob, even though I didn't have a clue what I wanted to tell him.

The call connected after one ring. "Hi Mr. Bob, this is an Angela," I said in a clear tone.

"Is everything okay?" Bob asked.

"I'm in over my head with the family business and could use some help," I told him.

"Are you home?" Bob asked.

"Yes." That was all I said. I didn't know how much information I should say over the phone, and I'd watched enough movies to be paranoid.

"I'm on my way," Bob said and hang up.

"It's going to be okay, right?" I asked the cats for moral support.

"Meow," they both replied.

I sat on the floor and leaned against my bed, closing my eyes. It was time to get myself together. I couldn't keep running away every time somebody attacked me. I couldn't keep hiding from Todd and his Barbie fiancée.

Bonnie and Clyde jumped on my lap and I wrapped my arms around them. Their soft purrs filled the room, and I found myself dozing off to the sound.

"Angela, dinner," a voice said in the distance.

I opened my eyes and found I'd fallen asleep on the floor. The room was dark, and I struggled to find my phone. When I finally got it, it was almost five. How was that possible? I jumped up and saw Bonnie and Clyde on the bed looking as comfortable as ever.

"Why didn't you wake me?" I asked the cats, who just rolled over on their bellies.

I ran to my bathroom to make sure I didn't have drool on my

face before walking back out. Five minutes later, I was back in the world of the living and rushing to the living room. When I got there, I just stood there. I had no clue what I'd missed, but the room was jumping with activity.

"There you are honey. I reheated your food," Minnie told me, grabbing me by the arm and dragging me to the kitchen.

"Hi, Mr. Bob," I said as I passed Bob. He sat on the couch with Andres, Julio, and Hector. I wondered what time he'd arrived.

"Hi, dear," Bob told me. "I have no idea where you found this boy, but he is a genius." Bob said, patting Andres on the back. Andres actually started blushing but didn't look up from the computer.

Minnie handed me a plate with lasagna, garlic bread, and salad. I took my plate and made myself comfortable at the kitchen table. Mother and Ethel joined us in the kitchen/dining area, but nobody said a word.

Everyone watched me eat, which made me pretty uncomfortable. After I took a few bites, I finally asked, "What did I miss and why didn't anyone get me up when Bob got here?"

"You had a long day, dear," Ethel told me.

"I had a long day?" Was she serious? "I wasn't the one who got evicted. Why are you all so calm?" Maybe I was still dreaming? Or maybe I was stuck in a parallel universe or something.

"It was a trying morning, but we have seen worse," Minnie told me with a smile.

"Ordering guns from the Russians to frame your ex," Bob said when he came in the room.

I dropped my fork on my plate and the Silver Hair Gang went silent. Mother started fidgeting with her buttons but didn't move. We held our collective breaths, waiting for Bob to pass his verdict.

"It's about time you teach that two-timing-good-for-nothing asshole a lesson," Bob announced, and we all let out a long sigh of relief. "Come here honey. You know your dad would be so proud." He embraced me before I was able to get out of my chair.

"My dad would be proud that I became an arms dealer?" I was a little taken back by that.

"Why do you think he left you his stash?" Bob said. "He said one day you would leave that loser and decide to do something with your life. The guns are there to help. You can do whatever you like with them."

"Can we pull this off?" I asked Bob.

"Absolutely dear. The hard part is done," Bob told me. "The guns have been ordered and are on their way to my ranch. The U-Haul has been arranged. Everything else is semantics."

"Where is Florence?" I asked, glancing around the room.

"Getting some supplies," Mother told me.

"Finish your food. We have a lot to do and not a lot of time," Bob told me. "We need to lock in the rest of your plan and make sure we have perfect alibis for you Monday. Everyone ready to get to work?" His eyes sparkled with excitement, and it made him look twenty years younger.

"I can eat and work," I told Bob as I grabbed my plate to head to the living room, but Bob pushed me gently back in my chair.

"Enjoy your food and relax," Bob said, crouching down to put himself eye level with me. "I promised your dad I would be here to help you if you ever asked me. I never wished this life for you and neither did your dad, but you are good at it. Make the most money and then get out just like we did, clear?"

"Yes," I answered in a whisper.

"You are not alone," Bob said. "Now eat so you don't pass out on us. We don't need a weak leader." He squeezed my cheeks, something he hadn't done in years.

I turned back to my plate and ate, slow and steady. This meal might be my last, so I decided to treat it that way. It changed everything. Each bite was an explosion of flavor. The sauce on the meat had a spice to it, but the cheese balanced it out. The perfectly cooked pasta and garlic bread added an extra layer of goodness. I listened to the conversation taking place in the living room. The people in there didn't sound defeated. They sounded like people fighting to survive.

We were all fighting back, and we were doing it in style.

Chapter Twenty-Four

𝓘t appeared Bob was more than just a weapons expert. He was also an incredible strategist. He thought of everything, even things we'd never considered. To pull this off, we were going to need some help. Everyone on the team had assignments that had to be done over the weekend, which made the days fly by in a blur.

Friday's Zumba class was packed. The word was spreading faster than we could've imagined and even Ms. Joyce came in. She brought spiced rum cake to share and it was to die for. Mother arranged to stand next to her during the session and enlist her services. The Silver Hair Gang made a fabulous appearance as assistants to Jesus. They ensured the whole crowd knew how Todd had kicked them out but what a blessing it was. Now they didn't have to keep any more secrets out of respect for his family, and of course me.

The rumor mill was going nuts all day Friday. According to Bob, it was crucial that people saw me around town like I owned the placed. I needed to ensure that everyone knew I held no ill will towards Todd, and that his rumors hadn't angered me in the least. It might've been the hardest thing I'd ever done, and it was also driving me nuts, but fortunately the boys came up with a better plan. We travelled through town, talking as loud as we could about all the exciting things we were doing. We went from the library, to the senior center, and even to the general store, all on foot. The plan was simple: I'd get supplies for the school while the boys spoke about how great everything was going all while the world eavesdropped. Not a difficult task in Sunshine since everyone made it their hobby to listen to everyone else.

At first, the process was awkward, but it didn't take long for Julio and Hector to get into character. By the time we were done, they had the whole town talking about our amazing school program, the great classes we were adding, and how fun and happy I was. We even made a quick detour by the administration building to drop off flyers in case other kids needed an alternative program. I was drained. I wished I knew computer stuff because I would have traded places with Andres in a heartbeat. His job was to create a digital trail of all the nasty stuff Todd had been doing.

Thankfully, Saturday did not involve talking to people. We were supposed to recon the drop point for Monday. Bob had a few ideas he wanted to incorporate and things that needed to be transported to the location. Minnie was good friends with the employees from the Corps of Engineer that worked at the dam. We had no idea how she did it, but she was able to get a map of the location. We needed to make sure we knew how to get in and out of the lake area as quickly as possible. I couldn't believe it, but this insane plan was actually coming together.

Sunday was delivery day. Bob pretended to work for Todd. Once the guns were secured on his farm, the rest of us went to work. We weren't planning to give up all the guns because that would be a waste. Every box had to be repackaged and half of the weapons were removed. We filled the boxes with enough rocks, wood, or plastic material to have the same weight as the original shipment. The process was a lot slower than we expected since we had to ensure we were wiping down fingerprints as we went. The U-Haul was packed and ready for our Monday adventure. We couldn't drop of the truck ahead of the meeting, though. It would only arouse suspicions, and we couldn't have any of that.

Monday was D-Day and I wasn't sure if I was ready. My stomach jolted inside me, and sharp pains assaulted my sides. I had a feeling it stemmed from my jittery nerves, and if I was a weaker person, I'd turn around and forget everything. Only, I wasn't anymore, and there was no turning back now.

At five am we had a pre-battle meeting in my living room. Mother, Ethel, Florence, Minnie, Bob, Julio, Hector, Andres, and even Maria were present. By the looks of the dark circles under the group's eyes, lack of sleep ran fluent in all our lives at the moment.

"Let's go over the plan one more time," Bob told us.

"Ethel, Florence, Minnie, Maria, Angela, and I will be at the senior center by six am helping Joyce serve food," Mother told the group. "Here you go ladies." She handed us a red and white striped shirt, a skirt, and floppy red hats. The senior center was having free breakfast for all seniors who arrived between six and nine thirty. The place was going to be packed, so there'd be plenty of witnesses to our whereabouts. Perfect.

"I have the Sheriff's department and the two-timing Todd," Andres said, rubbing his hands together. "I'll make sure to get them all there at the right time." I did not want to know how Andres planned to pull it all off, but if anyone could do it, he could.

"Tony and I will be driving the U-Haul to the location," Hector announced.

"Make sure to get out of there as soon as you park the truck," I told Hector.

"I will be on the boat, ready to take everyone to the rally point at Bob's," Julio said softly.

"Angela, are you sure you are ready?" Bob asked me.

"As ready as I'm going to be," I replied.

This entire plan depended on me and how quickly I could sell the guns. I was terrified but I was more afraid of spending the rest of my life trapped in this house hiding. It was time to go big because failure was not an option.

"Ladies, go change. It's time to make some money," Bob told us.

Mother, Florence, Ethel, Minnie, Maria, and I made it to the senior center at five fifty. Nobody told me the criminal life involved early mornings. This was a lot of commitment on our part. We rushed to the kitchen to find Joyce and eight other ladies wearing identical uniforms to ours. The floppy hats covered most of our hair and you had to look close to see the person's face.

"What do you think, Barbara?" Joyce asked Mother as they gave each other a huge hug.

"Perfect, absolutely perfect," Mother replied.

"Okay ladies, we have a busy morning, at least until nine o'clock, so look alive." Joyce handed us each a list of all the things that needed done before the doors opened.

We each ran to the large dining area to set up. Joyce stayed in the kitchen and put the finishing touches on her meal. The center was offering scrambled eggs, bacon, and biscuits and gravy. They also had cereal bowls and muffins for anyone who wanted something different, which was a rarity when Joyce cooked. Her food was to die for.

I found myself lost in my duties. All the chairs were placed on top of the tables each night. We had to lower the chairs, check the salt and pepper, refill the napkin containers, and make sure all the coffee carafes were full. I hadn't been expecting a huge crowd at six in the morning, but I couldn't have been more wrong.

The doors opened and over thirty people marched in. Every red-dressed helper got busy. Once the patrons arrived, our mission was to bring them their plates, drinks, and anything else they needed. According to Mother, my main mission was to make sure as many people saw me as possible. I had to make a point to greet people, and to help them with anything I could. Free food had a way of making people friendly, especially if it was being served to them. I made it a point to stop by every table at least once, as I carried coffee.

At around six thirty, I gave my carafe to Maria and snuck out the back with Minnie, who was helping with dishes. Minnie drove in her usual style, as fast as possible, while I changed in the car. I had a pair of pants and a sweater with running shoes. I didn't bother taking off the stockings since I had to put this getup back on as soon as I finished.

Minnie made it to the Overlook Point in record time. She always enjoyed driving fast, but today she had extra motivation. We needed to be in place before Billy and his boys showed up.

As soon as Minnie dropped me off next to the U-Haul, she took off. Luckily, I managed to get my phone out of the car before she drove off. I jogged to the end of the parking lot where Hector and Tony were waiting for me in the truck.

"I like this new look, Ms. Angela. It makes you look dangerous," Tony told me with a smile in his eyes.

"Good morning to you too, Tony," I replied. "Is everything ready?" I asked Hector as I inspected the crates they had laid out.

"Just like we planned," Hector replied. His job was to get us extra help. He recruited Tony, the only potential criminal we knew.

I moved between each of the seven crates the boys had set up. The lids were still on some of them, that way Billy and his boys would have to do some of the work. Hector and Tony both wore gloves, ensuring they wouldn't leave any prints on anything.

"Looks good, you two better get going before they get here," I told them.

"Are you sure we can't stay?" Hector asked.

"We talked about it. We need them to have their guards down and underestimate the helpless little woman." I gave them the sweetest smile I could muster.

"There is nothing helpless about you, and they are fools if they believe that," Tony said with a smirk.

"They will," I told him. "Don't come back unless you hear three gun shots in a row," I told them both.

"Yes ma'am," Hector agreed. "Here you go." He handed me the Smith and Wesson he had tucked in the back of his pants.

"Thank you," I told him and did a quick inspection of my gun.

"You need this," Tony handed me a pair of thin leather gloves from his pocket. "Would hate for you to leave your little prints after all the cleaning we have done."

"Good point, thank you," I told Tony and quickly put on the gloves. "Go," I told them and they both took off at a quick sprint towards the back of the creek, heading to the tree line.

This part of the creek had some beach areas for people to go swimming. It also had a little pier, perfect for small boats to be loaded and unloaded. Bringing Bob's fishing boat out there had been our Saturday project. It was hiding behind the trees on the water. We didn't want Billy and his group to figure out how I was leaving the place.

I watched the boys jog away until they faded behind the tree lines. It wasn't a very long distance, but I needed to make sure I went exactly where they did. That was the crucial part, otherwise I would be too far from the boat.

When I turned back around to check the boxes, the sound of vehicles pulled my attention. Right on time, two trucks pulled up. I slowly backed away from the boxes and leaned against the U-Haul. Billy was back, and he'd brought his three thugs with him again.

They all got out of their respective trucks and made their way over. It was interesting how all three were wearing low-key clothing and nothing flashy.

Billy's trio stopped near the first crate closest to them, while Billy kept coming towards me. "Well Ms. Cat Lady, I see you've been busy," Billy announced with a tone too sweet to be real.

"Here is my part of the deal. Now where is yours?" I asked Billy. We never negotiated prices, so I had no idea what he was bringing.

"I hope you don't mind if we inspect our cargo?" he asked.

"Be my guest," I said in a calm tone.

Billy gave a hand signal and his three henchman spread out, checking each crate. I pretended to be bored, picking at my nail polish while I snuck in glances every now and then. Plus, the nail polish wouldn't get ruined. Maria had given us all fresh manicures, that way we had matching polish. It just made me look a little ditzy.

It didn't take long for the group to finish searching, and they didn't do a very thorough job. I guessed they never expected anyone to double cross them.

"Satisfied?" I asked Billy once the trio joined us again.

"Nice work. Russian issued." Billy pressed his lips together and nodded. "I'm impressed. This is definitely the start of a beautiful partnership." He slowly strolled with a predatory grace.

"One-time deal, remember?" I asked him. "Where is my money?"

"Why in such a hurry? We could have some fun," Billy told me in that silky tone of his that made you feel dirty just by being near him.

I really didn't have time for these boys today, so I pulled out my faithful companion and pointed it at him.

"Sorry, darling," I said in my thickest Southern accent. "It's a little too early to play games. My money, if you please. I got places to go."

Billy wasn't afraid, but at least he wasn't getting any closer. His henchmen were ready to pull out their weapons and fire.

"Next time, then," Billy said and snapped his finger. One of his boys disappeared behind his truck, and reappeared carrying a suitcase, which he handed to Billy. In turn, Billy tried to hand it to me. "Here go you."

I shook my head. "If you don't mind, I'd like you to open it, please," I told him in a sweet voice. Truthfully, I planned to inspect my money, and to make a show of doing it just like they did with my guns. Plus, making sure his briefcase wasn't booby trapped wouldn't be a bad idea, either. Last thing I needed was my head blown off because of a bomb.

Billy gave me a closed-lip smirk, but his left eye started to twitch. He was not used to not getting his way. The henchman placed the briefcase on top of one of the crates and Billy popped it open. He turned it around slowly, and I made sure to plaster a big smile on my face.

"Do you mind?" I asked Billy as I motioned with my hands for him to back away.

"Of course," Billy replied as he backed up about five feet.

I did a quick inspection to make sure we at least had real cash in there. I had no clue how much money was in the case, but the surface was covered in Benjamins. I was hoping the rest of the stacks were packed with real money—the opposite of what we'd done with the guns.

"Thank you for your business. I hope I never see you again," I told Billy and gave him a head nod.

"You will," Billy replied, but I ignored him as I turned around and headed towards the water front. "Aren't you taking your U-Haul?" Billy called after me.

"Not today," I replied and kept on walking. If I heard steps following after me, the plan was to open fire.

I cut across the parking lot and nobody followed. By the time I reached the road by the water, my walk had turned into a jog. I risked a glance behind me, but still nobody followed. Then, I took off at a full sprint. I breathed a sigh of relief when I reached the boys.

Thank you, Father, I sent a silent prayer to the Lord as I tried to catch my breath. I was really out of shape. According to Bob, this was the easy part. Timing was going to be everything for the second part. As soon as the boys saw me, Julio was supposed to contact Andres. Bob had a nephew that worked in the Sheriff's Office for Cass County. Andres was supposed to call and report some suspicious activity by the lake while Bob's nephew was on duty.

"I got you," Tony told me as he pulled me onto the boat. As soon as I was on board, Julio lifted the anchor and shoved us away from the shore.

"Okay everyone, hit the deck and stay down," Tony announced as he took over steering the boat.

From my strange vantage point, it was a gorgeous morning. I could see the sun coming up over the water and the colors mixing with the morning sky. It wasn't bright enough for us to stick out on the lake, but we didn't want to take any chances. Tony maneuvered the boat around the lake. Bob was waiting for us a bit further down the lake at Lakeside Park. It was an easy five-minute boat ride to Bob. Tony was going fairly slowly, though, that way he wouldn't attract too much attention.

When we finally made it to the park, Bob sat by the shore with his fishing pole.

"Perfect timing," Bob said when I finally made it to land.

"Did the sheriff make it here already?" I asked, looking over Bob's shoulder at the road behind him.

"Not yet," Bob replied with a smile. "Nephew just texted and he is on his way, but just saw Todd's Lexus flying by."

"There is no way he is that dumb." I said.

"Either he is, or his plastic fiancé is, but one or both is heading towards our arms dealers," Bob said. "I told you Andres was good."

"I never denied that," I told Bob as I handed him the briefcase.

Julio and Hector had filled me in on how Andres had been communicating with Todd's fiancé all weekend regarding a secret meeting I was going to have with James. Andres promised the meeting was going to be compromising, and if they made it there in time, they could get some juicy pictures. I guessed their rumor campaign wasn't bad enough, now they wanted proof. Andres pretended to be a concerned citizen that lived on the same street as I did.

The boys and Tony were bringing in the boat, and Bob had his trailer ready to load so we could all head back.

"Tony, you and Angela need to head back," Bob told us. "We can handle the boat."

Julio and Hector both gave me a thumbs up, and for some reason the gesture made my paranoia rise to the surface. Usually when a teenager looked that happy, they were up to no good.

"Let's go," Tony said, and we jumped in a Nissan sitting next to Bob's truck. "Nice job, Ms. Angela. Not bad for a Cat Lady."

"Not bad at all," I replied and couldn't help but laugh. I buckled up and leaned back in my seat.

Fortunately for me, Tony was driving the speed limit. We didn't need to get pulled over on our way from the Lake.

We didn't speak much during the drive. but it was a comfortable silence. The kind you have with a trusted friend or ally. This was definitely a new twist for me.

Chapter Twenty-Five

The transaction at the lake took a lot longer than we'd expected and I feared people had started noticing my absence. Tony pulled to the back of the senior center and dropped me as close to Minnie's car as possible. I jumped out of one car and right into another and changed. Tony was a true gentleman, getting out of the car and leaning against the window of Minnie's car to offer me some form of privacy. I felt like a school girl, dressing in the back of cars. Less than two minutes later, I was back in my candy-striper uniform. I tapped on the window and Tony moved out of the way.

"Ten thirty at your place?" Tony asked.

"Yes, and make sure to tell everyone you are there for the buffet. Got it?" I told Tony as I headed back inside the building.

"Got it," Tony said as he jumped in the car.

The place was still madness inside. I'd texted Mother in the car to let her know I was on my way, and as soon as the back door opened, she ushered Maria into the kitchen. I grabbed the carafe from her.

I made a few rounds before speaking to anyone.

"We need more coffee over here," Joyce yelled from across the room.

"I'm on my way," I yelled back, and several patrons noticed me. The ones who didn't I made sure to wave at and get their attention.

One of the older gentlemen grabbed my hand and stopped me. "Angela, dear, I've been meaning to tell you all morning how great you look."

"I bet you say that to all the girls, Mr. Johnson," I told the flirty old man and pinched his cheeks. It worked! If Mr. Johnson believed he had been watching me all morning, then surely everyone else did too.

I made my way across the hall, pouring coffee along the way. By the time I reached Joyce, at least ten more people had arrived.

"I thought the place was going to start slowing down by now," I told Joyce.

"Blame your mother," Joyce told me in a hushed voice.

"Do I want to know what she did?" I asked, peering over my shoulder to make sure nobody was listening to us.

"She and her crazy ladies," Joyce started.

"The Silver Hair Gang?" I said.

"Yes!" Joyce exclaimed. "That is a perfect name for them."

"You can thank Julio and Hector for that one. I can't stop calling them that now," I told Joyce. "Please, tell your story. I'm sorry I keep interrupting you."

"They texted everyone at the retirement community, plus everyone else they know, and told them we are doing pie raffles during breakfast." Joyce frowned as she shook her head.

"You've got to be kidding," I said.

"Of course not," Joyce said, keeping her voice low. "I had to bake five pies for this crazy raffle. I'm killing your mother. I want my Zumba classes free for the next month." She jutted her chin out and planted her hands on her hips.

"Anything you want, Ms. Joyce," I told her and gave her a kiss on the cheek. "But you just reminded me we have Zumba classes at nine thirty and the only one home is Andres. We have to go." I raised my voice as loud as possible for the last part while still making sure I sounded kind of normal.

This was the cue to exit while the whole crowd watched. I rushed across the hall, waving at everyone as I went. I found Mother at the far side, organizing the pies and making sure the tickets were in order for the drawing.

"Mother, have you seen the time?" I asked her, making big hand gestures.

"Sorry dear, but no. I've been busy," Mother said in a big voice. "What time is it?" she asked me, but she also looked at her watch.

"We have Zumba class at the house," I told her.

Mother should have been an actress. All sorts of emotions crossed her face in a matter of seconds, from shock, to worry, and finally to panic. I had no idea how she did it, but a look of alarm crossed her face as her gaze roamed the room. She found one of the candy-striper volunteers and handed her the tickets with a quick explanation.

"Joyce, dear," Mother shouted from across the room. "We have to go, late for Zumba." She waved at Joyce, who graciously put her hand over heart.

"You guys better hurry. Thank you so much for all of you showing up today," Joyce replied to Mother, and then she waved.

Mother wasted no time dragging me towards me the kitchen. She waved to all the people working and went straight to the back. Florence, Ethel, and Maria were already in one car. They took off as soon as we came out. Minnie waited for us in the other one. I jumped in the back and Mother took the passenger seat. Minnie barely waited for the doors to close before taking off.

"How did it go?" Mother asked, taking off her hat as Minnie maneuvered through the parking lot.

"We got the money, they have the guns, and hopefully the Sheriff's department has them all," I told them.

"All in a day's work," Minnie told us.

I was exhausted, so I laid in the backseat for a short nap. My adrenaline was gone, and I was depleted.

"Don't forget to wake me when we get home," I mumbled to Mother. I couldn't afford another three-hour nap in this car.

"Of course, dear. We got more work to do," Mother told me. Her words didn't make me feel any better.

I was pretty sure Mother and Minnie let me sleep longer than the drive to the house. We were not fifteen minutes away, but I was grateful for the time. Cars were already lined up down the street. By the time I stepped out of the car, Jesus's music blared from the backyard, so I bustled inside, waving at everyone I passed on my way.

Andres and Julio were in the living room staring at the computer when I entered the room.

"Great, you guys made it back. What are you two doing?" I asked the duo.

"Trying to load more music to Julio's playlist," Andres said, and he gave the most dramatic eye roll I'd ever seen. "The regulars are complaining they have been hearing the same songs this whole time." Andres mocked air quotation marks when he said "regular" and "same songs".

"What's the problem again?" I asked him. I wasn't really following the reason behind his annoyance.

"This is only day four, so how can anyone be a regular?" Andres waved his hands in the air.

"Good point." He made sense. I'd give him that.

"Not to mention, all the songs are in Spanish, so how do they know that it's the same song?" Julio added. "They don't speak Spanish, right? But still, everything sounds the same to them!"

I had to turn around before I started laughing. We just finished a major arms deal, but somehow song selection was the issue throwing the boys over the edge. We needed to work on their priorities.

"Both of you need to breathe," I ordered them. "Just find some songs and let the people be happy. I need to change," I told them, and I ran to my bedroom.

Bonnie and Clyde were napping on the bed like they owned the place. I gave them a quick kiss on their heads, and like twins, they both wiped the kiss away with their paws. There was no winning with these cats. If I didn't acknowledge them, they were mad, and if I did, they were annoyed. Go figure.

When I made it back to the living room, the boys had already fixed the song problem and the class had started, so I darted to the patio to join the crowd. The backyard was unrecognizable. In the last couple of days, Jesus had made improvements to the place. He'd built a large work out area out of stone. The place looked like a tropical dance club. Around the edge of the dance floor he'd added benches, and even a sitting area. The place was adorned with tropical flowers and plants. Mother had told Jesus to make the space his and have fun with it. I was afraid to find out how much this "fun" had cost me.

With a shake of my head, I found a space near the back, which also happened to be close to the food table.

As soon as Maria and Hector arrived with the food, I jumped off the dance floor and started helping. As soon as the crowd smelled the food, they were salivating. Jesus took the hint and the music stopped, allowing the hungry crowd to march over to the food table.

People often took the help for granted, not noticing them at all. The thirty minutes after Zumba were the most informative. According to the rumor mill, Todd and his fiancé were arrested early this morning after being involved in a fire fight with some smugglers. The rumors became progressively more exciting. Some said that the smugglers had hit Todd's fiancé. Others said one of the smugglers was injured. By the time everyone was gone, each story contradicted the previous one.

Tony had arrived on time. Unfortunately, his gun crates were the ones we were using as tables for the food.

"You are all about reusing stuff," Tony told me as he pointed at the crates.

"I just hate to waste," I admitted. "Besides, we needed a secure place to keep them until you were able to pick them up."

"In the back with the food is as safe as it gets," Tony concurred.

"Now we just have to wait for the crowd to clear," I told him. "I'm going inside to sit. My feet are killing me."

"I'm coming with you, I'm beat," Maria told me and the two of us went inside the house.

"He is being charged with tax evasion. How did you pull that off?" Mother asked Andres when Maria and I walked in.

The Silver Hair Gang's ears were turned up as they listened intently for Andres's answer.

"I didn't do much with that one," Andres told us. "That man had plenty of skeletons in his closet, so he pretty much made his own tomb. All I did was open the door to it by sending a copy to the Sheriff's office."

"Could you use your magic and make me an eBay store?" I asked Andres as I remembered my side business.

"Are you kidding me? Andres turned around to look at me. "After all I've done, you still question my skills?" He covered his face with his hands.

"Of course not," I told him, bowing down to the computer guru.

"Why do you need an eBay store anyways?" Maria asked.

"I've been telling people that's my side business," I replied.

"In that case, we need one now," Andres said. This new sense of urgency had him jumping right back to his computer. "What are you going to sell?"

"I have no clue," I admitted as everyone turned to look at me.

"Me!" Florence squealed from the back. "Could we sell homemade soaps, creams, and bath balms? They can be made from essential oils," she asked without a hint of facetiousness in her voice.

"Sure, why not? I replied. "But where are we getting the stuff from?" My skills definitely did not involve making any of that stuff.

"You are in luck, dear, Florence can make it all and more," Ethel told me.

"You go, Ms. Florence," Julio told her, giving her a high five.

"In that case, we probably need an Etsy store instead," Andres told us.

"Sure, go for it." I didn't care as long as we had something on there that we could pretend to promote.

"The Cat Lady Special is opening for business," Andres announced, and we all laughed.

By eleven o'clock, Tony and the extra Russian weapons were off the premises. By noon, just like Bob predicted, two inspectors from the police department were knocking at my door.

"Ma'am, do you know this man?" one of them asked me.

He had handed me a copy of the mugshot they took of Todd. I hadn't seen him in months, and he looked rough. He had gained weight and was starting to lose his hair. I almost didn't recognize him. While James looked handsome and polished, Todd kind of looked like Uncle Fester from the Addams family. I needed to give God an extra thank you for closing that door for me.

"Ma'am, did you hear me?" the inspector repeated.

"I'm sorry, I was distracted," I said honestly. "He is my ex-husband, but I almost didn't recognize him. It's been a while since I last saw him. Why?"

Bob had explained how I needed to play dumb the whole time, so I was doing just that.

"He is accusing you of framing him," the inspector told me. "Where were you this morning?"

"I was at the senior center helping with free breakfast Monday and then we rushed back for our Zumba class," I told the inspector as calmly as possible. "What exactly did I frame him of?" I asked a little softer, trying to show concern but not showing too much curiosity.

"Trafficking arms," the inspector said.

"Oh my!" I replied, and that was all I said.

"Could anyone collaborate your whereabouts?" he continued.

The interrogation lasted a good twenty minutes. He was very professional and calm. At the end, he apologized for wasting my time and left. This was the biggest scandal Sunshine had ever had and the gossipers were on the prowl. It appeared that an actual fire fight broke out and Todd shot Billy. Billy was in critical condition and not expected to make it. I felt sorry for him, but at the same time, deep down inside me, I was glad he might be gone, which made me feel like a horrible person.

The Silver Hair Gang blessed me with a huge gift when they'd volunteered to distribute all the information to the gossip channel. They would keep me posted in case something important actually happened.

Bob was in charge of laundering the money. I had no idea what that meant, but he was going to be gone for at least a week. Translation, I could relax on my patio and do my crossword puzzles in peace for a few days. This felt like a mini vacation.

Chapter Twenty-Six

It was Friday afternoon and I was kid free, Mother free, and even Silver Hair Gang free. Ethel had planned a field trip to the science museum in Dallas. Ethel, being the overachieving teacher that she was, had decided she needed to bring her lessons to life. That translated into a field trip with everyone. I was pretty sure it was an accident that they didn't include me, but I was not going to argue. I was so excited to be home alone that I considered running around the house naked, just because I could. I quickly nixed the idea for a nap day instead.

It had been almost five days since the 'event,' which was what the citizens of Sunshine were calling Todd's demise. The phones had finally stopped, so I could enjoy the calm and tranquility of my house again.

Based on the newspaper reports, little Todd had been busy. Todd went from low annoyances/mild irritation straight to public enemy number one. Besides not paying his taxes, Todd had embezzled his clients' assets. He had switched his practice to state manager and had made himself the custodian of many funds. The charges continued to pile up, and it appeared his little *Barbie* was part of the scam.

I was stretched out on the couch, reflecting on Todd's future, when my doorbell went off.

"Not again," I said to myself.

My first reaction was to ignore it and go back to napping. Unfortunately, Bonnie and Clyde were whining at the door. That got my attention. Maybe it was a Girl Scout selling cookies and I was missing the opportunity. I jumped from the couch and headed towards the door.

"This better be good," I told the cats.

"MEOWWW," replied Clyde.

"Right, we will see." I unlocked the door, trying to avoid the cats farting between my legs.

"I hope I'm not a disappointment," James told me as soon as I opened the door.

"Oh, sorry about that. I didn't realize people could hear me through the door," I told James as I looked down at myself. I was wearing socks, a pair of Capri pants, and a loose T-shirt.

"Only when you are close to the door," James informed me.

"Good to know. I'll make sure to step away from the door when shouting about people," I told James and he smiled. "Now, how can I help you?"

"I hope you don't mind, but I wanted to give you these," James handed me a bouquet of flowers he'd hidden behind his back.

"Those are beautiful, but what are they for?" I asked, holding my hands at my sides. Truthfully, I was afraid to take them.

"For helping with the competition," James said with a wicked smiled.

"I'm sorry. I had nothing to do with that." I held back my smile. No way would I confess any involvement to the county judge.

"Of course not," James told me, but he was still smiling. "Then just take the flowers as a friendly gesture." He pushed the flowers into one of my hands, giving me no choice but to take them.

"Thank you. They are beautiful," I said, and I meant that. They were the most vibrant fall colors, so full of life and comfort.

"I also wanted to ask you to dinner," James told me. I opened my mouth to protest, but before I could, he covered my lips with his fingers, and that touch sent flames from my head to my feet. "The elections are less than two weeks away. I would like to take you out afterwards if that's okay."

I wasn't sure what to say. I hadn't been on a date for over twenty years. "I don't know," I said, and those were the only words I could think to say.

"It's just dinner Angela, not a marriage proposal," James said in a gentle voice as he inched closer. "If you have a horrible time, I promise never to ask you again."

"Is been a while since I've been on a date. I guess I'm not sure I know what to do." My hands were sweating, and my heartrate was elevating. James needed to back up before the lightheaded feeling he incited out of me took me down to the ground.

"That sounds perfect. I haven't been on a date in forever

either," James confessed with a grin. "We can figure it out together and finally understand what everyone is so excited about it."

"I think it's the meal, but I could be wrong." I was rambling and had no idea what I was saying.

"That's a great place to start. I keep eating the same things over and over, so this would give me a chance to try something new," James said, moving even closer. So close now I could smell his cologne, and it did things I didn't want to say out loud to me.

"Sure, dinner sounds great," I finally said. "I just hope you are not too disappointed in the company."

"Trust me, I won't be," James said and kissed my cheek. "See you in two weeks, Ms. Cat Lady. Have a great day," he said as he turned and walk way.

"You too," I said as I watched him, and I had to admit the view was nice.

I closed the door in what felt like slow motion, still thinking of his lips on my cheeks. I slowly touched my faced with the tip off my fingers. My body was ready to float away, so I leaned against the door.

"Am I really going on a date with James?" I asked the cats as I made my way back to the couch.

"He kissed my cheeks," I told the cats, staring at them as they followed me.

"MEOWWW," Bonnie sang.

I looked at my cats and quickly sobered up, "Damn!" I actually cursed. "He called me Cat Lady."

My heart was racing at full speed. What did this mean? I wanted to call him back and cancel the date, or maybe call Mother. Panic had settled over me in a rush, so I took several deep breaths and sat down. If he wanted to arrest me, he wouldn't have brought flowers. My life was getting more complicated by the minute.

I stood and stepped to the kitchen to put the flowers in water. As crazy as the idea sounded, and even with everything that was at stake, I couldn't help but be excited. More excited than I'd been in a long, long time.

"Cat Lady is going on a date with the county judge. What would the Silver Hair Gang say?" I told the cats. "Scandalous!"

The end for now, but don't miss the next installment in the Cat Lady Trilogy, A Desperate Cat Lady!

For up to date promotions and release dates of upcoming books, sign up for the latest news here:
www.dcgomez-author.com

www.bookbug.com/author-d-c-gomez

www.Facebook.com/dcgomez.author

www.Instagram.com/dc.gomez

www.goodreads.com/dcgomez

Acknowledgements

After twenty years of running away from my passion, I finally became brave enough to start writing again and publishing to hopefully motivate others to live their dreams. So, I would like to start by thanking YOU, for reading this book. Thank you for giving Ms. Angela a chance to become your friend and for cheering her on while she finds her way back home. I pray you are living your dreams, and if you are not, may you find your way back to them like I did.

I'm blessed with a great support system that always helps bring my books to life. Thank you to my family: my parents, brothers, sisters-in-law, and my best friend and better half for supporting me even when my dreams are all over the place. Thanks to my Texarkana community (I'm counting all my friends and family in all the surrounding areas here) that continues to support me beyond all my dreams. To my community in Salem for all their love throughout the decades and embracing this journey with me.

A huge thanks goes to one special angel that continues to blow my mind with her talent and passion, the talented Cassandra Fear. Thank you for being the most supportive editor and an amazing cover designer. Ms. Angela looks fabulous. Thank you to the talented Ms. Courtney Shockey, formatter extraordinaire. Thank you for putting all the pieces together and giving me a product ready to publish. Absolutely, it takes a village to get this done.

As an undercover cat lady myself, I couldn't conclude this book without giving thanks to my own furry assistant. Thank you Chincha for making sure Mom doesn't work too hard and we get plenty of breaks.

Once again, thank you my dear readers. If you managed to read all the way to this point you are officially my hero and I'm highly impressed. If you loved the book and have a moment to spare, I would really appreciate a short review as this helps new readers find my books. Help me spread the word!

About the Author

D. C. Gomez was born in the Dominican Republic and at the age of ten moved with her family to Salem, Massachusetts. After eight years in the magical "Witch City," she moved to New York City to attend college. D. C. enrolled at New York University to study film and television. In her junior year of college, she had an epiphany. She was young, naive, and knew nothing about the world or people. In an effort to expand her horizons and be able to create stories about humanity, she joined the US Army. She proudly served for four years. Those experiences shaped her life. Her quirky, and sometimes morbid, sense of humor was developed. She has a love for those who served and the families that support them. She currently lives in the quaint city of Wake Village, Texas, with her furry roommate, Chincha.